"FIND YOUR WILD"

Copyright 2016 by Pierce

Publisher: Pierce

First Edition: June 2016

Print ISBN: 978-0-9976441-0-4

Cover Design by Cover Couture (www.bookcovercouture.com)

Photo Copyright: nenetus/Dollar Photo Club

Back cover image "Black Satin" by iStock/Getty Images.

Lyrics of "Goodnight Romeo" by Phil Ayoub used by permission.

Formatted by E-book Formatting Fairies (e-bookformattingfairies.blogspot.com).

Contact Vanessa at xoxVKxox@gmail.com

Follow Vanessa Kincaid on Facebook, Pinterest, and Twitter.

Official book website www.learningjillian.com

# Sending Many Thanks To:

Dr. Neil Toback, dark chocolate and astrological counsel, for keeping me on a productive healthy cacao buzz and making sure I am compliant with the Universe.

Phil Ayoub, official VK erotic novel consultant, for sharing his song "Goodnight Romeo" and his invaluable baseball expertise. We'll leave it at that.

Giacomo, my cosmic big brother, for his unwavering support in all my projects past and present. I reiterate my vow publicly to never ever share this book cover, plot, or anything else about the "filth" with you except for financial business thingys.

Maggie McCormick, editor goddess, for cleaning up all my typed dirty thoughts.

My Master Beta Readers: Lisa Wagenbach, Amy Williams, Nancy Ramsdell, Maureen Philbin, Francesca Russo Barnes. Grateful for your time, input, and sordid minds.

You, my reader, I'd like to thank you for buying an authorized copy of this book and respecting intellectual property. Welcome aboard the Vanessa Kincaid love train. Please fasten your seat belt securely...but only if you're into that.

*Enjoy yourself,*
*xoxVK*

*Dedicated to the creator of men's baseball pants.*
*Thank you.*

# LEARNING
# JILLIAN

## ONE GAME AT A TIME

EMPOWER YOUR FLOWER COLLECTION

# ONE

Perched on the back of an orange armchair, a little white dog stares out a picture window. Her eyes widen when she spies something moving outside and begins to bark like crazy.

"Mimi, knock it off," Jillian Miles lovingly scolds her from the sofa without looking up from her romance novel. The fluffy West Highland Terrier ignores her and yaps continuously; the only thing that matters is what's in the parking lot below.

"I said knock it off," she warns this time, turning the page. *Must be a cat.*

While Jillian struggles to focus on her story, Mimi frantically hops about the chair, barking at whatever, or whomever, has captivated her.

Frustrated that she can't concentrate on a single word, Jillian lets out a long sigh. She tosses the happily-ever-after read onto the coffee table, accidentally knocking over her favorite mug; a green tea river gushes across the mosaic-tiled top. She jumps to her feet to rescue the book before the Starbucks tsunami drenches it. *Too late.*

"Damn it," she curses, picking up the dripping paperback. The yapping ratchets up yet another notch and sends Jillian over the edge. "Miiiiiimi!" she screams.

Exasperated at this point, Jillian leaves the sopping-wet mess and stomps over to the crazed Westie and the window. "Good thing you're cute. What on Earth is out there?" she demands, scooping up Mimi in her arms which at last silences her.

The two gaze out the large glass pane. Jillian scans the apartment complex grounds for what's interrupted her lazy Sunday--but sees only cars parked under trees bursting with New England Autumn color. "Nothing. For all that noise, there's nothing out there." She peers down at big brown eyes. "Are you losing it, Kiddo?"

Jillian places the Westie back down on the cushy chair and wags a finger at Mimi's wet nose. "Now be a good girl and be quiet."

After Jillian cleans up the spill, she plops her over-forty body back down onto the shabby-chic sofa, fluffs up its pillows, and gets herself comfy for an overdue nap. Content and relaxed in the perfect position, Jillian closes her eyes. *Finally some peace and quiet.*

Mimi jumps off the chair with a thud and runs to the door, whimpering to go out.

"You can't be serious," Jillian utters in dismay.

Mimi whines again.

Jillian opens her eyes to see the determined Westie taking a firm stance.

"Meems, you're killing me."

The little pooch scratches on the door.

Knowing there will be no other outcome, she gets up.

"Let's go," she surrenders to Mimi who darts in circles, all fired up.

As she heads toward the door, she stops to check herself out in the mirror. *Pathetic, Jillian.* She tucks the faded t-shirt, the one she can't part with despite its holes, into her worn-out baggy jeans. She frowns at her less than fashionable reflection. *At least there aren't any stains.*

"Who's gonna see me anyway?" she shrugs it off, pulling her ash blonde hair into a straggly ponytail.

Jillian leashes Mimi and the two step out into an unusually warm October afternoon. They stroll down the parking lot when, without warning, Mimi makes a sharp detour and yanks Jillian over to the back of a red Jeep Cherokee with its hatch open. Stacks of boxes and plastic tubs fill the trunk. *Somebody's moving in today.*

Mimi stands up on her hind legs, sniffing and scratching frantically at the cargo.

"Stop it," Jillian urges in a whisper but Mimi claws even harder until she inadvertently knocks a cardboard box out of the jeep; it lands upside down on the ground. Jillian is beside herself.

"What is with you today? Mimi, sit!" she orders under her breath. Detecting her owner means business, the little furry dog obeys. "That's a good girl. Now stay, I have to hurry and pick this up before the owner comes back."

She quickly flips the box right side up, but a little too fast--all of its contents fly out onto the pavement. She stands horrified that now a stranger's personal stuff lies scattered all about her feet: sports stick deodorant, shaving cream and razors, and men's underwear. *This is so not happening.*

She grabs as much as she can with the one hand not holding the leash and begins stuffing everything back into the empty carton when a handsome male face pops up between boxes in the rear hatch and startles her.

"Hey! Who's back there messin' with my gear?" he jokes with a dazzling smile before vanishing as suddenly as he appeared.

She's mortified. "Now you've done it," she says in a hushed voice to Mimi. "Pet World has a trade-in deal today: two cats for one nosy little dog. You better be good," Jillian swears as that face between the boxes, and the rest of him in body-hugging sports tee and shorts, reappears and stands next to her.

*Oh. My. God. He's hot.*

"I'm so sorry," Jillian apologizes nervously, flustered by his sudden appearance—and incredibly muscular physique.

"No worries," he reassures her with a calm sweetness.

After he lobs all the toiletries back into the open carton, Jillian watches him roll up every pair of underwear then perfectly pitch each one into his cardboard target. *What I wouldn't give to see him in a pair of those...as if...he's soooo out of your league.*

When Jillian turns away to sneak a peek at his belongings in the Cherokee, she doesn't see him eye the forgotten item still in her hand, or her.

"If you want to keep those, go ahead, they're not my favorite," he offers tugging at his waistband with a smirk. "Too snug."

Jillian peers down at the pair of black boxer briefs clenched in her fist. His briefs. *Oh please just let me die right now.* She can't make eye contact when she hands them back to him.

"Sorry," she squeaks, barely getting the word out. He bites down on his bottom lip to stop a grin.

Mimi again barks for something inside the jeep, "Cut it out," Jillian shushes her without success.

"So this must be our little culprit," he bends down to pet her head, but she doesn't stop moving long enough to let him. "Ahhh, hold on, bet I know what she's lookin' for," he says before dashing off to the front of the Cherokee.

Mimi keeps up her high-strung antics until a Fox Terrier bounds around the shiny bumper anxious to meet her. Sniffing and chasing each other in circles, the two dogs get acquainted when the square-jawed, chocolate-eyed hottie returns and leans casually against his 4x4 ride. He lifts up his baseball cap, runs his fingers through his brown locks, then nestles the red cap back on, firmly adjusting the visor over his chiseled-cheekbone profile.

Jillian catches him give her a once over twice and self-consciously tucks a loose tendril of hair behind her ear. *It figures I've just met the most beautiful man I've ever seen looking like crap.*

A scuttle breaks out between the dogs and diverts their attention; the amorous Fox Terrier tries his best to mount Mimi who will have none of it and bites at his tiny black nose. The would-be-suitor yelps and runs behind his daddy for protection.

"Dude, what did you expect? You didn't even introduce yourself first!" His buff owner laughs, patting the rejected Romeo. "Baxter, meet...?" he prompts Jillian with a questioning stare.

"Mimi," she replies, fighting off the butterflies flapping in her stomach from staring into his eyes a bit too long.

"Now go say you're sorry to our new neighbor," he coaches Baxter who romps back over to his white furry friend. Nose to nose, both canine tails wag amidst a long awkward silence between their owners.

"Are you guys moving in?" Jillian blurts out not knowing what else to say.

"Kinda looks like it, huh?" he ribs her. Jillian rolls her eyes at her stupid question and fakes a grin. *He must think I'm an absolute idiot. I am.*

Mr. All-American then stands up tall, all six feet two inches of him, and close enough to her that her heart pounds without her brain's permission. "I'm Dallas, by the way," he says while taking another box out of the jeep.

"Like in Texas?" she quizzes, trying to hide her sudden awareness of his broad shoulders as he places the carton on the ground.

"Yeah, but I grew up in Virginia," he explains in a way that says he's been asked that a million times. "The Monroes are a big sports family. Dad's a huge Cowboys fan. You?"

"Oh, I don't know anything about football," she answers sheepishly.

He chuckles and asks in a sincere voice, "No, I meant your name."

Her cheeks blaze fifty shades of pink once again. *Can I make more of an ass of myself with this guy?*

"Jillian."

"Sweet name," he smiles, cocking his head. "Suits you."

A male voice bellows from the building, "Hey Kid, ain't got all day. Get a move on!"

"Alright, alright, I'm on it," Dallas shouts back and waves up to a burly man leaning out of a second-storey window.

"The Cowboys fan?"

Dallas shakes his head no. "Uncle Jack. My nearest and dearest here in Boston. He's always got my back."

As Dallas unloads the last of his packed up-belongings out of the trunk, Jillian watches his quads and hamstrings flex to perfection. She tries, but can't peel her eyes off his torso and pumped-up arms that scream gym rat. *I'd bet everything he's got six-pack under that shirt.* When he bends over to place the last container on the ground, his deliciously-round cheeks posture up in the air right in front of her like two fresh melons. *No Photoshop needed for that butt.*

All of a sudden, without warning, Dallas does an about-face and Jillian prays she's looked away in time before getting caught staring at his ass. She didn't. He smiles knowingly.

"Do you live in this building?"

"Yeah, down at the other end."

"Cool. We'll have to make a play date then."

Jillian's face lights up and looks over at the two dogs who have become fast friends. "I think Mimi and Baxter would love a play date," she gushes, admiring them both before turning back to Dallas with an innocent smile.

"Who's talking about the dogs?" he quips in a sexy teasing voice and spins his baseball cap visor backwards.

Jillian's jaw drops. He flashes his best bad boy grin. She turns beet red.

"Kid, c'mon! Love can wait. I can't," Uncle Jack demands as he props open the apartment building door.

"Catch ya later, Jillian," Dallas promises as he lifts up a stack of plastic tubs and walks off towards his new apartment with Baxter scurrying behind him.

Jillian watches Dallas for awhile then shakes off her attraction. *Get a hold of yourself, he's wayyyyyy too fast for you.*

"Meems, let's go," she says to the Westie who trots along beside her with an ever-so-pleased-with-herself look across her whiskered face. "I know, I know...I owe you."

# TWO

The next morning, Jillian makes sure she's got everything she needs in her tote bag for work:

Laptop power cord? Check.

Thumb drive with client files? Check.

Diet salty snacks to balance out the ridiculously sinful afternoon chocolate treat? Double check.

*Okay. Good to go.*

Picking up her keys she calls over to Mimi stretched out on the sofa in the sun, "What if you go to work today and I stay home on the couch?" Mimi doesn't budge an inch. "Be good, I won't be home late."

Outside the crisp Autumn air feels wonderful. *Best time of year.* Walking over to her car, she spies her handsome new neighbor at the grassy end of their building throwing a ball for little Baxter who races madly to retrieve it. Each time the little guy brings it back, Dallas overly dramatizes his achievement to a happy wagging tail. *They're having a blast.*

Dallas sees her and gives her a big friendly wave. "Have a good day, " he shouts. She waves back and gets in her car. *I certainly will now.*

# THREE

"Of course he meant it! Men don't joke about 'play dates'," Jillian's Baby Boomer office mate, Josephine, exaggerates loudly like she always does when she's excited about something. "Why can't you just believe he's interested in you?"

Jillian slumps doubtfully in her computer chair. She picks at the pilling on her cashmere cardigan.

"Maybe because he's about ten years younger than me and I'm about ten pounds overweight?" she downplays Josephine's enthusiasm and grabs at her belly. "Only thing I got from the divorce. Anyway, I'm sure he flirts like that with everyone."

Josephine waves her chubby arms madly in the air which jingle her Cable Channel Shopping crystal bangles and jostle the black ringlets from her recent spiral perm.

"Oh, please. Give the guy some credit, would you? He sees you're a natural beauty, even if you can't. If you don't go out with him so I can live vicariously through you, I swear to The Hoff," she threatens Jillian before pressing her palms together in prayer in front of a glossy Baywatch photo of David Hasselhoff posted above her monitor.

Jillian chuckles. "This guy's a great fantasy. But in real life? No way. I'm sure he's into hookups and wild women. That's just not my speed. To be honest, Jo, I only had one boyfriend before marrying Greg. And neither of them had that kind of body...nor a trapeze over the bed, if you know what I mean."

Josephine blinks, her mouth gaping wide open. "Only two men? Two?"

Jillian nods, her lack of experience making her uncomfortable.

"Honey, if I had your figure and blue eyes, I'd have two men before lunch."

A balding man in khaki trousers and polo shirt sticks his head into the cubicle, "We're back online, ladies. Might be slow, but at least we're up and running."

"Russ, if you weren't married," Josephine jokes with him and he shoots an index finger gun back at her. "When is Phasitech going to upgrade? Seriously, PAC-Man is more cutting edge."

"Workin' on it, Josie. We'll be here late tonight to make up for the lost morning. If either of you need anything, page me, okay?" Russ drums his hands on the cubicle partition before walking off.

"Thanks, Russ," they both chime in after him and reboot their computers.

Josephine isn't about to let Jillian off the romance hook, "If he asks you, just promise me you'll think about going out with, wait, what's his name?"

"Dallas Monroe."

Josie clutches the edge of her desk with one hand and her ample-bosomed chest with the other. She stares at Jillian with full-round eyes. "His name is Dallas? Like in Debbie Does?" she demands in a near yell before pretending to faint.

Jillian leans forward in a belly laugh, worried that half her workplace just overheard Josephine who is spinning round and round in her chair, fanning herself with a memo.

# FOUR

Later that night, Jillian drives her car into the last parking spot in front of her apartment complex and shuts off the lights. *Thank God this day is over. All I want to do is crash.* She gets out, locks the door, and heads toward her apartment.

Half-way there her stomach rumbles. *Dammit I should've picked something up to eat. I wonder if the supermarket is still open?* She dredges the bottom of her oversize handbag for her cell phone. *I can't see a damn thing out here.* Engrossed in her search, she doesn't notice the man standing nearby in the shadows.

"Just getting home?" the hidden stranger asks.

Jillian jumps and instinctively clutches her bag close to her body.

"Who's there?" she blurts out in fear, her heart in her throat. She scans the dark lot in a panic.

A familiar furry face scampers into the light and towards her. *Baxter.* Dallas steps out of the blackness, the lime green fluorescent strips of his track suit glowing. The wild thumping in her chest slows as she pets the terrier's scruffy head.

"Sorry, I didn't mean to scare you," he apologizes with concern.

"It's okay," she replies catching her breath. "How are you?"

"Good, thanks."

"All settled in?"

"Pretty much."

Baxter gets greedy for more of her affection.

"Hey, Bax, give the lady a break." He whistles and the terrier obediently runs over to him.

The outdoor lights of the apartment building accentuate his sweaty his forehead as Dallas pulls one ankle up behind his butt to stretch out his quads. *He must've gone for a run.*

When he lunges side to side, his manly post-jog scent--that unmistakable smell of testosterone--floats into her nostrils. She happily breathes him in. *Mmmm...Eau d'Athlete.* Jillian's pulse begins to race again, but now for an entirely different reason.

"Do you always work so late?" he asks.

"Our server went down this morning, we had to make up the time."

"Technology's only good when it works," he empathizes while loosening up his calves. She can't stop herself from following the lines of his ultra-defined legs which protrude proudly through the thin sports fabric.

"That's for sure," Jillian concurs.

Dallas bends down and grabs his toes for a good hamstring stretch; his upper back muscles ripple between well-developed shoulders. Then with palms down on the pavement, he rocks his pelvis side to side. Jillian's body heat rises in an instant. *I can't take this.* She forcibly pulls her gaze away from this younger fitness god and instead searches for her cell once more.

Dallas stands back up and twists out his taut obliques.

"Hey, why don't you come over tonight and catch the big game with me?" he asks casually.

Jillian, shocked, looks up at him. *Did you really just ask me that?*

"Big game?" is all she can manage to babble.

"You're killing me. You know...game seven of the playoffs?"

Jillian shrugs her shoulders and gives him a blank look.

"Boston Cougars and New York Pirates?" he exaggerates his disbelief with a boatload of charm.

"That's baseball, right?" Jillian hams up her ignorance.

Dallas chuckles and keeps on,"Yeah, and the winner tonight goes on to...," he tries to coax the right answer out of her but she plays dumb. "...every baseball player's dream? The Pennant Race? Please tell me you've at least heard of that," he begs with his hands.

"Yes," she giggles.

"Whew. Good. Ever watched one?"

She shakes her head no.

"Wow. Okay," Dallas says to her then looks down at his tri-colored buddy, "Bax, we've got a lot to teach this girl." Dallas looks back up at her. "You realize now this means you have to come over tonight."

Jillian fidgets. *Alone with you? And that body? In your apartment? Any woman would go in a heartbeat...any woman except me, the big chicken that is Jillian Miles...no, I just can't. Be polite and talk your way out of this--before you're in over your inexperienced head.*

"Thanks, but I'm really beat," she says playing up her physical exhaustion, which isn't all that much of a lie.

"And you're starving right?" he asks.

She agrees, shooting him a look begging for sympathy for her long hard day. "Yeah, I should try to get the market before it closes." She thinks she's successfully thrown him off track.

"Problem solved. I'm ordering pizza for the game. You won't have to cook a thing."

*Damn, he's good at this...of course he is.* Jillian stares down at her Mary Janes, timid but torn. Little does she realize that her body language tells him she's within an inch of caving in to her attraction.

Dallas whips his baseball cap visor forward and salutes her while standing at military attention.

"I promise I'll make doubly sure the toilet seat is clean and down at all times, Ma'am."

Jillian lets out a hearty laugh.

Dallas relaxes his pose with a soft smile. He slides his hands into his track pants pockets, looks her dead in the eye with total honesty, and speaks in a small voice, "Look, Jilly, I could really use the company. How 'bout it?"

She doesn't know what to say and looks off into the parking lot as if she'd find the answer out there somewhere. *He's sweet... and seems kind of lonely, actually...and how often does a guy like this ask me out?...he seems harmless enough and the walls are paper thin if there's any trouble...I'll just go, watch the game, then bolt home right after it's over.*

She faces Dallas with a new confidence, albeit a thimbleful.

"No anchovies," she firmly insists with a twinkle in her eyes. Dallas beams.

"No anchovies," he promises. "I'm in 214. See you in twenty or so?" he asks, his energy all of sudden revved up.

"See you then."

# FIVE

A heap of clothes lies on the floor in front Jillian's reflection in a full-length mirror. In a hurry, she tries on yet another top. *You look like a frumpy old lady in that.* She takes it off and hurls it on top of the pile.

Jillian checks the clock. *Shit, I've only got five minutes.* She runs to the closet and back with another armful of possibilities. Mimi watches her like she's nuts.

Her phone rings as she pulls on a buttery-soft denim mini. Jillian zips up the skirt and picks up her cell to see the caller ID. *Josephine. Thank God.*

She answers while pulling on a dusty blue sweater. "I need your help," Jillian pleads and puts her on speaker phone so she can try on shoes.

"What's wrong? Are you alright?"

"Dallas invited me over to his apartment to watch the baseball game."

"Geez Louise, you really had me scared there for a minute," Josephine chastises her before shifting into dating coach mode. "But this is great news, what's the problem?"

"What if this is just a hook up? I'm not capable of that, especially with a guy like Dallas," Jillian sputters, worked up into a tizzy.

"You gotta relax, sweetie. You think too much. Just look at this as an opportunity to get to know each other. Go enjoy yourself."

"Well, I would like to get to know him better, but," Jillian says, her voice speeding up from an oncoming anxiety attack.

"But what? Jillian, what's this really about?" Josephine pries with kid gloves.

"If we do it, he'll find out I don't know my ass from his elbow in bed. That's why Greg left me for the bimbo, right? I can't go through that again." Jillian then goes dead silent.

"Honey," Josephine sympathizes before Jillian cuts her off briskly.

"I think I should cancel. This just ends badly."

"Greg's an ass and you're not canceling. You're getting way too ahead of yourself here. It's a baseball game, not a marriage proposal. Want some advice?"

"Please."

"Just go, don't overthink it, and keep your panties on. Can you do that?"

Jillian takes a deep breath. "I think so. Yes."

"Good answer. You just saved me a trip over there to smack you if you said no."

Jillian giggles. "Any last piece of wisdom?"

After a pause, Josephine responds, "Sit in a chair facing him and not next to him on the couch. It'll give you more space to relax and be in control of the situation. Got it?"

"I feel like I'm in the seventh grade."

"We never really leave junior high, darlin', that's one of life's biggest secrets."

"Thanks, Josephine. I should go, I'm already late. Wish me luck."

"Have a great time. Can't wait to hear all about it tomorrow. Go Boston!"

# SIX

Jillian walks down the hallway, her nerves growing with each door she passes, until she finds 214. Dallas's loud TV bleeds through the wall. From the pounding in her temples, she is sure her blood pressure is ten times higher than normal.

*What am I doing? I've never done this. I should just leave right now, go home, and make my excuses when I run into him again.* Jillian looks down the hall, back toward the safety of her apartment. *And tomorrow Josephine will kill me...and I may never get another chance with Dallas if I blow him off tonight.*

Jillian knocks daintily on the door. Baxter barks.

"It's open," Dallas shouts from inside.

She adjusts her sweater and primps her hair. *Go in and aim right for the chair. You'll be in total control and everything will be fine.* She pushes the door open and steps into his apartment with as much bravado as she can muster.

"Hey. Glad you made it. I had my doubts," he jokes. "Take a seat, we're in the bottom of the first."

Jillian looks around the spacious living room and her confidence sinks all the way down into her ballerina flats.

*There's no chair.*

*There's no anything.*

The room is dim and nearly empty; nothing on the walls, no furniture, only a flat screen TV propped up on a box near a futon mattress in the middle of the wall-to-wall carpeted floor—with a shirtless Dallas Monroe lying on top of it.

*Oh Dear God.*

Dallas rolls over onto his side, his bottom half molded into black athletic tights, and smooths out his sheets to make a spot for her. "Don't worry, I made sure they're clean."

"Safe at third!" the TV sports announcer screams and fans go wild causing Dallas to pivot his full attention to the screen.

Jillian, frozen in place by the door, takes in the sparse room—and the backside of practically naked Dallas cheering the play.

*Just go, don't overthink it, and keep your panties on, she said.*

She digs deep to push herself out of her comfort zone. She slips out of her shoes and tiptoes barefoot over to the futon.

While Dallas pumps his fist with gusto at the TV, Jillian surveys her tiny allotted sitting area and carefully slinks down into it. She squirms to find a comfortable way to sit that won't flash him her undies when he turns around. *Why did I have to wear a short skirt?* After several unbearable positions, she relents to sitting cross-legged and stretches the denim mini over her lap as much as she can. *So much for space to relax in and be in control.*

The Boston fans go wild when their Cougars player hits a home run. Dallas is ecstatic. He claps and whistles at the TV before rolling over onto his back, resting an inch away from her bare legs. His nearness heightens her anxiousness, and her simmering arousal.

"That was awesome, huh? Pure baseball magic," he says, smiling up at her.

She returns the smile with a quick nod, all the while aware of her rigid posture. *He so knows I'm a wreck right now.*

Colored light from the TV flickers over his ripped abs and defines the lines of his clean-shaven pecs as he laces his fingers underneath his head. *He's a centerfold dream...get it together, Jillian, you're here now and you're gonna have to lighten up...as much as you can on a near stranger's bed.*

"So, is your decorator on strike or are you into the Minimalist look?" she razzes him.

Pleasantly surprised by her zing, his face blossoms into a Cheshire Cat grin. His eyes convey exactly what he's thinking about her—and she knows for damn sure that in this thought she's not wearing any clothes. She pretends to watch the game to keep herself together.

"I move around a lot. No sense in getting fancy."

"For work?" she asks frankly, returning to make eye contact with Dallas but instead finds him peeking at her panties. Jillian tries nonchalantly to pull the mini skirt down over her crotch, but this only brings more attention to it.

Enchanted by her shyness, he gives her a break and looks back up at her face which is noticeably blushing even in the low light. "I pitch. Minor league. In post-season I fill in for Uncle Jack's semi-pro teams up and down the East Coast. I go when and where I'm needed," Dallas explains, proud of his career.

"But don't you get tired of always living out of a box?" she asks, happy for a real conversation.

"Nah. It's been a habit for a long time. There's freedom in it," he says trying to convince her yet sounding more like he's trying to convince himself.

"Must be tough on your love life though," she digs subtly for personal history.

"Why's that?" he shoots back without any hint of emotion.

"Well, if you're never settled, how do you have a relationship?"

The intercom buzzes and she jolts. Baxter barks. Dallas looks relieved not to have to answer her question.

"Pizza guy," he rolls over and grabs his wallet from under the corner of the futon. He hops up and thumbs through cash in the billfold. His black leggings highlight every thigh muscle and curve of his butt—not to mention that hard-to-miss bulge in center field.

He pulls out some bills, goes to the door, presses the buzzer, then tosses the wallet onto the nearby galley kitchen counter. Dallas chats with the delivery guy about the game.

Meanwhile Jillian waits, fusses with her skirt, and scans the empty room. *No photos, no personal items...who is this guy? Does he have a girlfriend somewhere? Or a wife?*

After the door thuds, the sound of clinking bottles brings her back to the moment.

"Would you like a beer?" Dallas asks with his head in the fridge.

"No thanks."

Dallas struts back to the futon and drops the pizza box down in the middle of the mattress. He sits cross-legged mirroring her, and takes a sip of his Guinness before setting it down on the floor.

"Did I miss anything?" he asks, checking the TV for the score.

"I wasn't paying attention, sorry."

"Nope, still up by one. But bases are loaded, that's bad for Boston." They dive into the pizza, Baxter waits patiently for his portion.

"Why?"

"If the New York batter makes a base hit now, their third baseman could score a run and tie up the game; but if the batter hits a homer, all players on base score runs—sending Boston up Shit's Creek without a paddle."

"I get that," she says, pleased with herself for understanding. "This is good pizza, by the way, thanks."

"No problem." He tosses a chunk of crust to Baxter who chomps it down. "Hey, where's Mimi? You should've brought her. She must've been cooped up all day."

"I called my dog walker and she took her to the park around four. It's not cheap, but when I can't get home it's worth it. Mimi loves her! And she gets more exercise than when I take her out. She was dead to the world when I left," Jillian explains, finally starting to relax.

"I'm happy to walk her if you need somebody. Here, let me give you my number, just shoot me a text. It'll save you some cash," he offers and scribbles down his digits on a dirty pizza napkin.

"That's nice of you, thanks. I can do the same for Baxter," she counters as she takes the greasy paper from him.

"Cool. We'll swap keys once I get a spare," Dallas says as Jillian chews an overly-ambitious mouthful of cheesy pizza. "Then I can rifle through your underwear drawer while you're at work."

Jillian chokes on the pizza and starts to cough.

"Are you okay? I'm joking," he insists and grabs the nearly full bottle of beer and gives it to her to take a swig. She guzzles down half the Guinness in one shot to help dislodge the cheese and toppings stuck in the back of her throat. *Didn't do the trick. Need more.* She finishes the whole bottle of beer, her eyes watering and tears rolling down her cheeks from the ordeal. Eventually, she swallows it all down.

"I was kidding, Jilly," he reiterates with apology as he touches her leg. "Sure you're alright?" he removes his strong hand as she pulls herself back to normal. The heat of his touch lingers on her skin.

"Fine," she answers now feeling a little tipsy. Her runny mascara stings her eyes. *I must have eyeliner all down my face...oh, screw it, I don't care what I look like or being in control anymore...I like how his hand felt on me...so masculine...so caring...I like him.* She flashes him a sweet smile to let him know he didn't upset her.

"I'm curious about something," he states in a serious tone, reclining on his side, propped up on his elbow.

"Okay...what?" she responds tentatively.

"How has a woman as sexy and beautiful as you stayed so Virgin Mary?"

She stares at him as if every one of her fears is scribbled across her sweater in big black Sharpie. *I knew he'd see right through me... this is my worst nightmare come true...I should end this right now... but there's something about him...I like him, he makes me feel safe... maybe it's the beer, but it feels okay to open up to this guy.*

"Growing up, my parents never talked about sex. Ever. It was this unsaid thing that sex was something a girl wasn't supposed to do, never mind enjoy. So when I got married at twenty-seven--"

Dallas cuts her off, flabbergasted, "Wait, you were a virgin until twenty-seven?"

"Not exactly. I had my first real boyfriend in college, but that didn't give me much experience."

"Was he blind? You're smokin' hot," Dallas questions her with his brow furrowed.

Jillian basks for a moment in his compliment. Comfortable with this beautiful and kind younger man, she decides to reveal things she's never told another soul.

"Senior year he came out of the closet to me. He just couldn't fake it with a woman anymore."

"Whoa. And you had no idea?"

"I had nothing to compare it to. He was a sweetheart--always considerate and gentle. I adored him. However, looking back at our most intimate rendezvous, it was pretty much rated PG, if you get my drift."

"Man, tough break. And sex with the husband?"

"It was nice, I guess. In the beginning."

"Nice? I've called sex a lot of things, but never 'nice'."

"He taught me stuff he liked, which was fun at first, but then it was always the same...year after year...until it was non-existent." Jillian's voice trails off.

Dallas downshifts into low gear. "Jilly, you have no idea what turns you on, do you?"

Horribly embarrassed, Jillian starts to get up. "I think I should leave, the beer is making me talk too much. I have work tomorrow. Thanks again for the pizza."

Dallas reaches over and places a sympathetic palm on her forearm to convince her to stay, "Wait up." She remains seated but clearly upset. He retracts his hand.

"It wasn't a put down, I wouldn't do that to you. What I meant was it just sounds like you've never had the chance to explore yourself sexually. And you deserve to. Everyone should."

The roar of the baseball crowd hijacks the room. Dallas and Jillian turn to the TV to watch as Boston clinches the playoff in an extra inning.

"Pennant Race, baby! Woohoo! Nice job, Beantown!" Dallas congratulates the television with a two-finger whistle.

He returns his gaze to an unglued Jillian. His eyes take in her innocent beauty while his mind seems to be hatching a plan. "Hey, I have an idea," he says with a sudden zeal.

"Dallas, just forget what I said," Jillian insists.

"No, no, here's what we're gonna do. I promised to teach you baseball, right? The Pennant Race is best-of-seven games. So we each pick a team. When my team wins, I choose the sex. You do as I ask--whatever, wherever, whenever I say. When yours wins, I'm at your mercy. However you want me. Winner of the series gets to choose a special trophy."

Jillian blushes. "Dallas, I can't." She looks away.

"Why not?" he fishes, sounding slightly wounded. "You must be into me or you wouldn't be here."

"I do like you, it's not that." She turns back to him, wanting him to believe her.

"Then what is it?" he pushes gingerly. Jillian can't utter a word. Dallas forges on regardless,"You don't know the real answer to that, do you? 'Can't' is just your default setting. It's time to step up to the plate, Jillian. You're a beautiful woman. Let me be the one to show how to play those games too."

"Dallas--"

"I know there's a part of you in there that's raring to come out. It's time." He looks at her with certainty. "Trust me with this. I'm your guy."

Jillian's eyes explore his runway model face. She wants to let go, wants to give in to him, but there's still an old thread of fear holding her back.

"Look, I can't guarantee I won't change my mind—or be able to please you in that department." She lobbies on his behalf--and for her own self-protection.

"You think too much. Start living in your body, not your head," he explains kindly.

This familiar mantra puts a smile back on her pretty face. *Josephine would so love you, Dallas.*

"So I've been told," she chuckles under her breath. "You sound like a friend of mine."

She sits silently, admiring the sincerity shining out of his tremendous eyes. *What a gorgeous person you are, Dallas Monroe, inside and out...you're right, it is time...and I think you are the one.*

And then, just like that, that string which had held her back all her life unravels and snaps. She places her hand on his knee and asks, "So, when is the first game?"

Dallas is a very happy man.

"In a couple of days, Friday night some time. Are you free?" he asks while reassuring her with a gentle squeeze of her hand.

"Yeah, I am. Let me know," she says in good faith. "But right now I really should get going."

"I hear ya, it's getting late. But can I ask one more thing before you go?" he quizzes, holding her gaze long enough to make her stomach flip.

"Okay," she responds shyly.

"I was wondering," he mutters in a low voice, watching his finger slowly trace an invisible line up her calf toward her knee. She inhales with a slight quiver. Donning a mischievous grin, he then circles her kneecap again and again with the soft pad of his thumb. His tantalizing touch gives her goosebumps which are visible to both of them.

"You were wondering what?" she asks in a breathy voice.

He leans in close to her and whispers, "Can I kiss you goodnight?"

There's nothing she wants more than to feel that exchange of sweet wetness between their lips, that bond of connection with him. "Yes," she answers in a whisper.

His mouth moves toward hers, leaving a trail of warm breath all along her cheek. She tilts her chin, shuts her eyes, waiting for their tender contact.

But the kiss never comes. Instead she feels him sliding the hem of her skirt up her thighs. She sucks in her lower lip to combat the instant hormonal rush now raging through her veins.

Jillian's eyes pop open and witness the crown of his brown locks face down in her lap.

"Dallas?" she blurts out between short bursts of shallow breathing. He doesn't reply--nor does he stop hiking her jean skirt up ever closer to her waist.

Instinctively she wants to lose her fingers in that luscious hair of his, grab hold of his magnificent shoulders--but despite what he's doing to her, she's too shy to touch him. With her heart thumping out of her rib cage, she shoves her palms down on each side of her hips and clenches up the sheets in tight fists.

With her mini skirt now at her midriff, Dallas runs his moist tongue up along the entire left side of the triangular patch of her dainty pink panties. His five o'clock stubble tickles and scratches the crease of her leg. It's blissful agony.

She presses her eyes shut to regain some control, yet this only increases the sensation of what's happening below. Jillian arches her back involuntarily when his tongue works its magic up the right side.

But it's when he darts the tip of his moist tongue in and out all across the top of her waistband that it's more pleasure than she's ever felt in her life; she grips the sheets as hard as she can all the while her body tingles with newfound joy.

Dallas's masterful tongue withdraws contact, but only so his lips can place a firm hot kiss in the center of that awakened triangle of passion.

He sits up with an air of satisfaction, leaving her thighs trembling. Her face begs him for an explanation. "You didn't say where to kiss you goodnight. First lesson: Be specific when telling your partner what you want." He winks and jumps up onto his feet. She can't form a sentence even if she wanted to.

He extends his hand to help her up. *He seriously expects me to be able to stand up right now? I am an absolute puddle of Jello.* Without a word, she accepts his strong hand, and wobbles up onto her feet.

Dallas swaggers on ahead toward the door. Baxter, who had slept through the whole baseball game, leaps up from his dog bed when he hears Dallas near the kitchen.

The little terrier bounds over to his master, zipping past Jillian who is making a futile attempt to get her shoes on. Somewhat self-conscious and still hot and bothered by what just happened between them, she slides on her flats and makes her way over to Dallas, still desiring that elusive first kiss.

But Dallas is all business. He opens the door for her and politely asks, "Shoot me text so I have your number? Then we can make the key swap. Cool?"

Jillian agrees but her feet won't budge. *I want you to kiss me. Now. On my lips. Specific enough?* She lingers there, hoping.

Dallas steps back to allow her room to walk out the door. She hesitates another second but finally resigns herself to the fact that the night is over.

"I'm glad we got together tonight," he says.

"Me too. Goodnight," she mumbles, reluctantly sauntering past him into the hall.

"See you soon, Jilly." He smiles and shuts the door.

She pauses there outside his place, reveling in what she just shared with Dallas Monroe. She looks at number 214 on the door. *Friday.*

# SEVEN

At her desk, Jillian stirs her daydream of Dallas around her mocha latte until Josephine flies into their cubicle.

"I swear every old lady in Boston was on the road this morning. I could've gotten here faster if I walked," she complains, unwrapping her scarf. "I'm dying to hear how it went last night."

Jillian smirks before raising her mug to her lips.

"Don't you dare keep me in suspense after I almost killed myself to get here for the Dallas debrief," Josephine threatens, air-slapping her with her gloves. Jillian giggles and puts the cup down.

"Well, I kept my panties on like you said, but," she concedes playfully.

"Oh goodie, that grin tells me there's more to this story. Let me get settled and then you'll have my full attention." Josephine hangs up her coat then sits down at her desk. "Good Morning, Studmuffin," she says, blowing a kiss to David Hasselhoff. She turns to Jillian with a commanding one-eyed stare. "Spill it."

Jillian gushes over the previous night's events with Josephine hanging on every word.

"Oh my God, I would've jumped his bones right then and there. I don't know how you didn't."

"I wanted to. Really wanted to. But I didn't know what to...Josephine, he compared me to the Virgin Mary. And it's so true. How on Earth am I going to get through seven games?"

"Sex Education, the only course I ever got an 'A' in back in high school. Time to get out your favorite porn movies and take notes."

Jillian's expression says it all. Josephine is surprised by her reaction at first, but realizes she shouldn't be.

"You don't have any, do you?"

Jillian sheepishly shakes her head no, "You do?"

"Hell yeah. My sisters and I collect them like Hummel figurines. But my mother is the worst; if a DVD goes missing from any of our stashes, we all know who's got it."

"Your mother?" Jillian gulps in disbelief.

"I'm gonna take a wild guess here, honey, but your mama's never watched "Thrust & Lust", has she?"

"Not unless Martha Stewart is in it."

"Bad visual," Josephine puts up her hand in protest. "Let's not go there." She scribbles something on a post it note and hands it to Jillian.

"What's this?"

"A good porn site. And my username and password. I know you won't pay to subscribe," Josephine needles her. "Take a look. It's got just about everything anyone can imagine. Get some ideas of what you might like—or what he might."

"Oh God, okay." Jillian swallows hard and stuffs the yellow paper in her purse. "I'll check it out," she says unconvincingly. "Thanks."

# EIGHT

*What's this?* Jillian juggles her armload of groceries, purse, and laptop to take down an envelope which is taped to her apartment door. *I don't recognize the handwriting, I hope it's not bad news.* She sticks the business size letter in her mouth while she unlocks the door and goes in.

Mimi bounces over to greet her. Jillian picks her up and the two sit together on the sofa while she opens the mystery envelope. Inside there's a key loose at the bottom and a document.

As she unfolds the official-looking letter, a scrap of paper falls out and onto Mimi's head. "Sorry," she offers the Westie as she picks it up. *This handwriting is so messy I can barely read it.*

Hey Jilly,
I was at the team doc's office today so I figured I'd get this out of the way. I'm clear fortake-off. I'm guessing you are too. The game starts at 8 on Friday. I'll grab some wine Text me red or white.
Cheers, Dallas

Jillian opens the folded carbon copy bearing a doctor's letterhead. *Negative for all STDs.*

"He knew I'd be worried," she says as she tickles Mimi's belly. "He's a pretty thoughtful guy, isn't he, Meems?"

She refolds the report and slides it back into the envelope then takes out his apartment key. *This is all getting too real—and fast. Only two days away. Am I ready for this?*

"Sweetie, I've got to get up," she says while pushing Mimi as best she can off her lap.

Jillian takes Josephine's post it note out of her purse and settles down at her computer. After logging in as her rambunctious colleague, she discovers a whole new world called Internet Porn.

Squeamish, she studies the list of movies to choose from: there's one with fake-breasted women in leather corsets whipping a man chained to a bed, and another with a woman kissing another woman yielding sex toys she never wanted to think about, let alone see. The titles go on and on.

Jillian finally clicks on one featuring a good looking athletic guy. Before the video starts however, her screen floods with XXX-rated pop ups. *Oh my God, make it stop!* The rapid-fire ads featuring raunchy sex acts continue to take over her browser, layering nasty porn shots one on top of the other. She panics and keeps hitting the escape button but can't get the explicit windows to quit loading. In desperation, she holds down the power button and forces her computer to shutdown. She closes the lid of the laptop fast to make sure the whole sex thing goes far far away.

*I. Can't. Do. This.*

Holding her head in her hands, Jillian resigns herself to the only thing she can do: Tell Dallas tomorrow that the whole thing is off.

# NINE

While reading a label of almond butter in the health food store, a person cuts rudely in front of Jillian to grab an item off the shelf. She looks up to discover the jerk is her ex-husband.

"Greg?" she gasps, shocked to run into him there of all places.

"Hi, Jillian. How are you," he says more than he asks, coldly pecking her on the cheek.

"Fine. Since when are you ever in a supermarket?"

"Kiki is out of town, so here I am fending for myself."

*Kiki.* Jillian stifles a catty glare behind her feigned smile. *Stripper convention?*

She peruses the items in his cart and points to a jar. "You're allergic to that. It gave you hives for a week."

"Oh, I didn't know," Greg says, quickly taking the cashew butter out of the basket and shoving it back on the shelf in front of them. "You saved me, thanks."

"You don't cook, why don't you just get take out?"

"She works most nights, so I've learned to make a few things. Take out gets dull after awhile."

"Why can't she make stuff ahead of time? I always had something in the freezer to heat up."

"I was really spoiled with your cooking, Jillian," he confesses with a hint of nostalgia in his voice. "To be honest with you, Kiki is a sexy woman but she can't cook a damn thing. I guess there's always a trade off."

*Asshole! I should've let you eat that whole damn jar and itch to death.*

Greg is oblivious that he just dissed her. "Well, I should get going. Good to see you." He walks off and she's stands fuming at him—and herself. *Just go get the broccoli and get out of here.*

As Jillian makes her way toward the busy check out counter, her cell phone vibrates in her pocket. Standing in line she takes it out to find a text message from Dallas, "Red or white?".

*Sorry, Dallas.* Jillian types a long excuse why she isn't going over to his place after all. She proofreads it before hitting send. *That's really lame.* She deletes it and shoves the phone back in her coat. She tries to think of something better to write while she places her groceries on the conveyor.

Through the big window behind the cashier, she catches a glimpse of Greg who is getting into his shiny BMW. Anger surges inside her. *Screw Greg. And screw Martha Stewart. I'm so done with being the Virgin Mary.*

She takes out her phone and texts back to Dallas, "Red".

# TEN

A deep crimson Merlot pours into Jillian's wine glass. Dallas then fills his own as she swirls the vintage red around in the crystal stemware she brought over. The Star Spangled Banner singer on the television belts it out.

She's about to take her first sip when he adamantly stops her. "Don't drink!"

"What's wrong?"

"We have to choose teams before the game starts. Bad juju," he insists. Dallas comically yet urgently ransacks the room for something. She, all smiles, watches him with delight.

"What are you looking for?" she asks.

"You didn't drink yet, did you?" he mockingly threatens.

"You better hurry, the guys with the red hats look like they're doing something important," she eggs him.

"No, no, no...wait! I know where it is," he says to himself aloud before racing into the next room, his bedroom. She hears a cardboard box being madly torn open. He sprints back in and holds out a quarter in his palm.

She squints curiously at him. "Why didn't you say so? I probably have one in my bag."

"My lucky quarter, totally different monkey," he blurts out and glances over at the TV. "Boston is taking the field, call it. Hurry! Heads or tails? "

"Hmmmm," she answers, stalling to get a rise out of his superstition.

"C'mon, c'mon, call it," he laughs. Both of them are enjoying this silly charade.

"Heads."

He flips the coin in the air, catches it, then slaps it down on the back of his hand. "Heads, you're sure?"

"Positive," she responds.

He lifts his hand and uncovers the quarter: Heads.

"Okay, choose your team."

"I gotta go Cougars."

"Knew you'd choose Boston. Alright, we're on. When the Cougars win, I'm all yours." They clink wine glasses just as the first batter steps up to the plate.

Dallas tastes his Merlot and eyeballs her head-to-toe from over the rim of his glass. She flips her hair back over her shoulder after she swallows and makes a clandestine survey of his tight jeans.

"Who's favored to win?" she asks as they get settled down on his futon to watch the game.

"St. Louis. In a sweep," he answers, sprouting a wily grin.

"Hey! No fair. You should've told me that."

"All's fair in love and baseball, schweet-haht," he taunts her. "By the way, how do you like this wine?"

"It's really good," she sounds pleasantly surprised. "I pegged you more as a micro-beer kinda guy."

"Why, 'cause I'm a jock?"

She fears she's offended him. "Dallas, I didn't mean--"

"I'm just playin' with you. My mother's family owns a vineyard out in Napa. I grew up with wine in my blood and on the table every night." Dallas shines with pride talking about her. "Mom taught me everything there is to know about good wine. She was crazy into it."

"Was?"

Dallas catches himself and veers into a matter-of-fact seriousness. He downs the rest of his Merlot, then starts to pour himself another glass.

"She died when I was a senior in high school."

"Oh, I'm so sorry."

"Thanks," Dallas says. "She never got to see me pitch for the division championship. But that's life, right?" He empties the last of the bottle into her glass.

The TV crowd goes crazy. Dallas, focused on the video replay, never sees Jillian analyzing his profile. *That must've been tough to lose his mom so young.*

"Yes!" Dallas shouts, happy with the umpire's call. "My Bishops are kicking your Cougars ass," he brags before lowering his voice into a deep male tone and licking his lips like a wolf about to pounce on its prey. "Might as well take my winnings now."

Without hesitation, he places his pitching hand on her inner thigh and gives it a good squeeze.

Jillian's heart races out of control but she refuses to let him see her flinch. She meets and holds his alpha gaze, staring right back into the dark brown salivating wolverine eyes across from her. She cups her two manicured hands around his almost too strong-grip of her leg and slides it from hers over onto his own.

"The game isn't over yet." She play-slaps the back of his hand.

His eyes mimic his primal grin and tell her he's more than turned on by her unexpected show of authority. The sexual tension between them is so thick she could spoon it up and lick it like gelato. Her insides shake like a leaf, but a sense of pride steadies her. *So far so good.*

Over the next hour, Jillian learns about line drives, double plays, and a bunch of other terms she hopes she won't ever get quizzed on.

By the eighth inning, her belly makes a loud noise. "I'm starving. What's for dinner?"

"Dinner? Oh, shit, didn't think of that. Pizza again? Chinese?"

"I'm shocked an athlete like you eats so much junk."

"I grab a salad at lunchtime," he defends himself. She shakes her head dismissing his reply.

"Do you like veggie lasagna?"

"Big time."

"I made one yesterday. I'll run over to my place and get some. We can reheat it here."

"That would be awesome," he says as he caresses her foot. "Better hurry, though, the way Boston's playing tonight, the game's gonna be over sooner than later...and then I'll have you too busy to eat. Well, lasagna anyway." He licks his bottom lip.

Jillian's nerves roar back full force. She can't look at him. "Set the oven at 350. I'll be right back."

In the hall outside his door, she stops for a moment, breathing deeply to regain her composure. She hears Dallas talking to Baxter, his loving voice tugs at her heartstrings. *You're doing fine.* She takes off down the corridor. *Hope I didn't use too much garlic.*

Twenty minutes later, Jillian slides her lasagna pan out of Dallas's oven while he uncorks another bottle of wine at the counter.

"That smells incredible," he drools.

"Thanks," she replies, happy she's pleased him.

She slices the lasagna and starts heaping two large portions onto warmed plates when the baseball fans on TV go insane. Dallas rushes to the edge of the galley to see what's happening.

Jillian looks up from grating parmesan to steal a look at that perfect ass hugged by his worn denim and broad muscular shoulders in his snug navy pullover. Dallas shouts at the television but she can't understand what he's saying. She turns back to her meal prep.

Dallas struts back over to her. "Well, no surprise, St. Louis won. Seven to two."

The unsaid fact that Dallas has just won hangs in the air. Jillian buries her gaze in the tossed salad, cowering now that her moment of truth has arrived.

"So I guess this means the Cougars won't be out partying tonight," she says meekly while sprinkling croutons. She feels her face flushing red and can't look at Dallas who hovers close by.

"Nope. They're probably heading for the showers right about now," he explains with a playful cocky tone. "And so are we."

Dallas smacks her hard on the ass. He pulls his sweater up and over his head and throws it on the floor with fuck-yeah dominance.

Jillian does a fast one-eighty toward a gloating Dallas. His direct stare down into her eyes fires up an intense storm--and desire--inside her.

"My win. Let's go," he commands, swaggering off toward the bathroom.

She looks over at the plates of steaming hot lasagna when she hears the shower stall door close. *But I didn't expect...now?... what about all the food?*

The sound of water running drowns out the TV post-game commentary.

*He's in there waiting for me.* Her eyes offer the food an apology. *Gotta go.*

She follows the trail of Dallas's discarded clothes to the bathroom: first his white t-shirt crumpled up in a ball, his jeans a few feet farther, and then his briefs, the same ones she handed back to him when they met, now tossed on the rug like her own personalized invitation to sex.

The door to the bathroom is wide open. Steam from the hot shower hangs like a cloud trapped between the tiled walls—and there, through the frosted glass shower door, stands a naked Dallas Monroe.

Jillian trembles as she pulls off her socks, unbuttons and wriggles off her jeans. She folds them neatly and then does the same with her blouse. *Quit stalling, Jillian, just drop them and get in there.*

She steps into his bathroom and catches her reflection in the foggy mirror. She watches herself unhook and remove her bra then slide off her panties. *Goodbye, Virgin Mary.*

She slides the shower door open. A dense wall of moist heat hits her face and envelops her body as she steps over the side of the bathtub. Through the humid fog, Dallas stands with his magnificent backside to her, moving his head to and fro under the shower head, enjoying the water cascading all down his Michelangelo physique.

The sudden cold draft and the clunk of the shower door closing causes Dallas to turn and face her.

*And there he is in all his naked glory, every inch of him.*

Jillian stands awkwardly at the far end of the tub not sure what to do.

He smiles tenderly at her from under his dripping locks which are plastered flat against his square jawline. *God, he's so beautiful.*

"Don't be shy." He extends his arms to her, his palms calling her into him. "C'mere, gorgeous."

She pushes her dampened hair away from her face and wades toward him through the shallow rapids swirling about her ankles. The spray from Niagara Falls behind him douses her as she slides into his slippery embrace.

As he pulls her close, Jillian wraps her arms around his six-pack, placing her hands on the arch of his back. *His skin is so warm and soft.* A split-second upon her touch, she feels Dallas shudder.

"Your hands are freakin' cold!" he roars loudly.

Dallas spins the two around placing Jillian under the shower head to warm her up, drenching her head to toe. She presses her eyelids shut to keep out the aquatic avalanche which only magnifies the sensations of the scalding river streaming down her body--and Dallas now kneading her ass.

When she reopens her eyes, she finds his locked onto hers with a hungry look she hadn't seen from him before. Water droplets dangle from his long dark eyelashes. He hugs her tighter, his warm wet body sliding against her closer than ever, and devours her mouth with his own under the rousing waterfall. They kiss well. Enveloped in a sensual mist, their tongues mingle to the sound of rushing water all around them.

When she feels his chin pull back, she reluctantly lets go of his lips. *Why is he stopping?* Dallas steps to the side of her, reaching for something. She blinks away the droplets from her eyelids, struggling to see what's going on.

Dallas, all smiles, hands her a bottle of body wash before he turns around so she she can start on his back. "Wash me...and don't forget to get behind the ears," he grins.

The steamy cloud above now threatens to fully engulf them as she rubs the soap between her hands, its sporty musk scent undeniably male. Jillian lathers her way up his spine in slow-moving circles, tracing each individual rib as it comes, then back down to the crest of his pelvis. Dallas exhales and raises his arms over his head and rests his interlaced fingers behind his neck. His enjoyment of her touch excites her, giving her more courage to explore him. With butterfly hands, she presses her thumbs on either side of his spine and follows the soapy trail all the way up to his neck.

"That feels so great, Jilly."

She scoops up some extra suds and grabs a firm butt cheek in each hand, cupping his powerful sexy glutes. Arousal for both of them rockets sky high.

Jillian slides a sudsy hand up one of his inner thighs and then the other while Dallas groans his pleasure. She pours more liquid soap into her palm and starts to lather his hips when he takes her hand and guides it around to the top of his washboard abs. She closes the gap between their bodies and presses her breasts into his back. He moans his approval.

"Touch me."

She kisses between his shoulder blades as her hand descends teasingly-slow down the front of his torso. His ever-deepening breaths reverberate under her lips.

The lines of his chiseled stomach eventually give way to a tuft of coarse hair. She pauses her hand there, fingering the tiny wet curls, hoping the wait will drive him crazy.

It does. Unable to contain his needs any longer, he guides her hand down onto his full length, teaching her grasp the rhythm that makes it sing.

"Yeah. Like that." He drops his hand and lets her take the wheel.

Jillian keeps steady on; he tilts his head back and lets out a bellowing groan. His left hand swings around behind her and grabs onto her ass. As she continues the tactile tempo his hand squeezes her butt so hard in response to his surging pleasure it's almost more than she can bear.

"Oh fuck yeah," he screams.

His body squirms uncontrollably as it nears Nirvana. Dallas suddenly slams on the brakes to avoid reaching that heavenly state too soon.

"Wait. Stop." Dallas jerks his body forward out of her reach. He pivots and faces her.

"Not yet," he barely forms the words between pants. "Turn." She obeys.

He squeezes an abundance of body wash into his hand, then steps closer, positioning himself right behind her.

Jillian catches her breath when she feels his excitement bob against her ass as he lathers her every curve. She leans her head back towards him as his large foamy mitts make slow circles up her belly and between her breasts.

His hands slide all down her arms to clasps hers. He raises their entwined fingers overhead planting her palms flat against the wet fiberglass stall. *I couldn't move if I wanted to.* With a deep voice he murmurs into her ear, "Keep 'em there."

He bends her body slightly forward with his own, placing her head directly under the shower faucet. The sheer force of the downpour rushing over her face disorients her: it floods her eyes, her mouth, she breathes some in and swallows a little more. For a moment she's transported to a tropical amazon rainforest—until his knee parts her legs and she feels Dallas thrust himself inside her.

Sensory overload. Drowning in a lagoon of sexual pleasure, her hands squeak against the shower wall as she is rocked forward and back by his forceful thrusts. The deluge from the Heavens muffle her moans and his grunts until the very last ones echo loudly throughout the tiled room..

He pulls her hands down as he releases himself from her, and not letting go of her hands, wraps his big arms around her and draws her close. They stand together in the hot misty fog, catching their breath and savoring their new level of intimacy.

Dallas pushes her hair back, wrings it out into a ponytail, and sees she's absolutely waterlogged. "Better get you outta here before you wrinkle up like a prune." Dallas reaches to turn off the water.

She stands like a fawn who has just successfully tested out her new legs.

"Hey. Look at me," he says with tenderness, aware of what a big deal this was for her. She gazes up at him. He takes her chin gently in his hand and says, "That was amazing." He kisses her sweetly.

Dallas throws open the stall door and jumps out of the tub. "Thank you, St. Louis!" he hollers.

Jillian laughs and climbs out of the stall. Now comfortably naked with him, and herself, she thoroughly enjoys mussing up his hair and wiping down his back with a big bath towel.

The room temperature cools down enough that Jillian starts to shiver uncontrollably.

"Here, get this around you." He swaddles her in a fluffy towel and dries her hair with a smaller one. She adores being taken care of by him.

Looking up at him all starry-eyed, Dallas bends down to kiss her wanting lips but instead asks, "So where's that lasagna? I'm starving!"

"Typical," she slaps his hip. "You're such a guy."

Later that evening, after the new lovers have eaten, they lie entangled on his futon dozing off. She, content and nearly asleep, curls up in the clean smell of his skin. Her own spent body feels completely relaxed and peaceful.

"Jilly," Dallas nudges her to wake up. She resists. "It's late. Want me to walk you home?"

*Are you kidding?* She stirs, not wanting to ever move from her cozy warm spot next to him. "I'll just stay here and get up early. Mimi will be fine," she says spooning into him and drifting back off.

Dallas carefully wrangles himself free and sits up. "Let's go, sleepyhead," he sing-songs before getting up.

"No, really, I'm good here," she mumbles with her eyes closed. "But come back down here."

"Come on, Jillian," he says in a tone that makes her realize he's serious. She opens her eyes and sees he's at odds with himself— or her.

"Did I do something wrong?" she questions, sitting up and rubbing her eyes.

Dallas shifts his weight back and forth, then kindly but firmly lets her know, "No, of course not. Tonight was great, Jilly, really, but it's just that I have a 'no sleepover' policy. Nothing personal."

*Nothing personal? How could kicking me out now not be personal?* Drowsy and not able to process this unexpected turn of events, Jillian gets up and starts getting dressed without saying anything.

Dallas walks up to her as she buttons up her blouse and puts his hand on the small of her back. "Hey, really, it's not you. It's just a space issue with me. Are we good?"

Jillian nods and reaches down for her loafers, not looking at him, not really knowing what to think.

"Let me walk you home?"

"No need," she brushes him off, just wanting her own space now. "Oh, my lasagna pan," she blurts out, the fact that the closeness between them has somehow disappeared makes her want to cry. *What happened?*

"I'll drop it off tomorrow, washed even," he tries to get to smile. She doesn't.

He takes her face in his palm and sincerity pours from his eyes, "Jillian. I think you're an amazing, beautiful, sexy woman. I just sleep alone. Okay?"

She wants his words to be true. "Okay."

He walks her to his door and kisses her one last time. "Sweet dreams, gorgeous."

# ELEVEN

"Helllllooooo, Earth to Jillian," Josephine tries for the second time to get her attention.

Begrudgingly, she puts aside her mind's replay footage of her exciting night with Dallas to bring her attention back to work. "Yes, Josephine, I'm listening."

"I can't seem to log in to anything. Can you?"

Jillian tries several times then gives up. "Nope, we're down again."

"For crying out loud. How am I supposed to meet my deadline tomorrow? That damn John Moran. Maybe if he put some of his CEO bonus money into buying a decent system we could get some work done around here."

"Owners never think that way."

"Yeah, well they should. I'd give him a piece of my mind if I ever met him. And a good swift kick in the ass."

Jillian chuckles, knowing she would. "Josephine, can I get your opinion on something?"

"Bet I know who this is about," she chides her. "Shoot."

"Last night was wonderful, but he wouldn't let me spend the night. Said he has a 'no sleepover policy'. I don't know what to think about that."

"Honey, guys, especially younger guys, like to keep things on the light side. No strings attached. Sleepovers make that tougher. Hate to say it, but probably for the best; I can tell you're already falling head over heels for him."

"How am I supposed to not have feelings for a man I've been that intimate with? He's so sweet and caring. And fun."

"And handsome. I get it. But you both know he's only here for a month at best. You got to keep your head on straight with this. You're not going to marry him, so just enjoy the honeymoon—it's usually the best part of a marriage anyway," she tries to cheer Jillian up.

But Jillian doesn't want to hear that, even though she knows deep down that Josephine is right. *This is why I can't handle hookups. If I like the guy enough to sleep with him, I want a relationship. I knew this would happen.*

Josephine's phone rings. "Hi Russ...alright, we'll go for an early lunch...let's hope it's a quick fix...good luck." She hangs up and tries to comfort an emotional Jillian, "Come on, let's go over to Mexicana Grille, my treat. You can fill me in on all the juicy parts of last night."

"Thanks, Josephine," she says smiling. "You're the best."

# TWELVE

After a long Sunday morning walk, Mimi and Jillian are wiped out. "We're almost home," she says to the little dog when Dallas's Cherokee cruises right past them and parks. Jillian is glad to see him, although still feels unsettled about their situation.

He waves then climbs out of the jeep, rocking a pair of jeans and unlaced construction boots. *What is it about untied boots on a man that makes them so sexy?*

"I've got great news!" he announces, brimming with excitement.

"You look happy, what's going on?" Jillian asks.

Dallas strides over, pets Mimi before kissing Jillian lightly on the lips. "Hey, gorgeous," he says in a low voice. Her insides melt. "So get this," he starts, his exhilaration bubbling over the top, "I got a call from a Fall Ball agent. There's a player who might go for surgery, I might get a chance to sub. How awesome is that?!"

"That's great news!" she echoes his contagious excitement. "What's Fall Ball?"

Dallas laughs. "It's off-season baseball out West. The best Minor League players get to play in front of all the big scouts. This could give me the biggest break of my career."

"Wow! When will you find out?"

"I have to try out first, meet with managers out there and stuff. Should get a call tomorrow if they're serious."

"So you'll be flying out to...?"

"Arizona. Probably a red eye flight. Man, I can't believe this, I am so stoked," his adrenalin is pumping so high he can't stand still.

"If you want, I can take Baxter while you're away."

"Oh, hadn't even thought of that. That would be great, Jilly. Thanks."

"No problem. You'll love that, won't you?" she says to Mimi.

"Speaking of loving," he says with a lustful tone, thrusting his hip up against hers and sliding his hand on her ass, "Game Two is tonight at eight. Are we on?"

Jillian drums up a sassy attitude to disguise any lingering disappointment from the night before, "We're on. But why don't you and Baxter come over to my place this time? I have furniture."

He squeezes her ass with appreciation for her dig at him. "Sure."

"I'll cook, you bring the wine. I'm going to need it after brunch today with my family."

"That's a deal." He plants a teaser of kiss on her. "Tell Mom I send my best." He winks and jogs off towards his place. She turns away dreamy-eyed but then pivots back when she hears him call out, "Oh, and just so you're ready, St. Louis is favored to win tonight three to one. Last night was just a warm up. Consider yourself warned."

She holds his cocky gaze and doesn't flinch, at least on the outside. "Don't be late."

# THIRTEEN

Jillian tries desperately to squelch all her thoughts of Dallas when she joins her conservative family for the obligatory Sunday brunch. At Chez Pierre, her mother, dressed to the nines, sits where she always does, opposite her father in his standard blue blazer and tie at the head of the elegant table. A constant pair for decades, her older sister Lauren and husband Ken sit side-by-side like Royal Doulton bookends. And then there's Jillian, who sits next to an empty chair, her most steady date at this weekly Miles Family function for the last five years.

After ordering their meals and general chit chat, her father clears his throat which shushes all conversation and draws everyone's attention to his announcement.

His voice switches from a dad to a politician when he says, "Glad you are all here. I wanted you all to be the first to know I've decided to throw my hat in the ring for re-election."

"That's terrific news," Jillian's older sister exclaims.

"Congratulations, Bill," Ken adds.

Jillian, not surprised that he's going for his sixth term in Congress, gives her blessing, "That's great, Dad."

"I'm glad you all approve. I'll be making my decision public at a fundraiser tomorrow afternoon. I'm hoping you all will be there."

Her mother answers decisively for all of them in her usual bossy style, "Of course they will, what could be more important than their father? I'll make sure everyone in the extended Miles family will be there in a show of support."

Ken wipes the corner of his mouth with a linen napkin seemingly to give more room for the spiteful smirk which follows. "Better make sure Morgan and his new girlfriend get the cue to stay off-camera."

Jillian's mother clucks her tongue, livid. "Your aunt is out of her mind over him dating that girl. What is he thinking?"

"I like Sasha," Jillian stands up for her cousin's girlfriend, but in a non-confrontational way. "She's sweet. Morgan is the happiest I've ever seen him."

Her family stares at her like she just committed murder. Jillian recoils from speaking her mind and hides in her English Breakfast teacup knowing she just stirred up a hornet's nest of negative opinions.

"She's trashy. Have you seen how she dresses? A young man like Morgan should be dating roses not dandelions," her mother snaps with a vinegar-laced tone.

*Dandelions?*

Her father agrees. "As the saying goes, "if it floats, flies, or," he pauses to adjust his vocabulary not to use a profane f-word, "Um, flirts, you rent it, you don't own it. Don't parade it around for the family and the public to see."

*It?*

"I'll call your sister, Bill, and have a word with her. Don't you worry," her mother reassures him.

Jillian keeps to herself for the rest of the meal, all the while imagining what they would do if they ever found out about her and her own sexy dandelion Dallas.

# FOURTEEN

"How are the yams coming along?" Jillian asks, opening her oven door. The smell of beef tenderloin floods the kitchen, making them both drool.

"Almost done, Captain," he promises and keeps chopping.

Jillian wipes her hands on her apron and inspects his progress. Having him in her kitchen while she cooks is almost as good as sex...well, okay, a far second, but it's next on the list. "You're not so bad with a knife."

"Okay, finished. What do I do with these?"

"In the pot on the stove, please."

"God, I'm hungry," he complains, scraping the orange vegetables into the stainless steel cookware.

"The French onion soup should be ready in about fifteen minutes."

"Good. I'll need all my strength for my win tonight. And so will you."

"Never give up on Boston," she counters and turns the dial up to high.

"And what will you do with me if you win?" he baits her from behind, putting his arms around her, kissing her neck as she stirs the soup. She doesn't resist.

His cell phone rings. "Dammit," he groans, pulling himself away from her to check the call. "Sorry, it's Uncle Jack, I have to take this," he apologizes then scoots into her living room. "Hey, Uncle Jack, any news?...Seriously?!" The pumped up pitcher lets out a whooping yell which makes both dogs bark.

Dallas rushes back into the kitchen. "They want to meet me!" he shouts, lifting Jillian up in the air and twirling her around and around. She laughs and screams with delight. "I got my shot!" He slides her down into his arms and gives her a juicy kiss.

"Dallas this is great. Congratulations. When do you leave?"

"In three hours."

"Three Hours?! So soon?"

"Uncle Jack got me on the next plane to Phoenix. I've waited all my life for this. I can't believe it."

"You'd better pack fast."

"Yeah, I should go. Sorry about dinner. And the game."

"Baxter will enjoy your beef," she taunts an overjoyed Dallas.

"You're killing me. Save me some? I'll be back in a couple of days, I think."

*You think?* It then dawns on Jillian that he might not come back at all. *What if they ask him to start right away? I'll lose him even sooner. Forever.*

"You should get going, Dallas, don't miss the plane. Let me know how it goes?"

"Will do. Keep your fingers crossed." He kisses her cheek then pets Baxter before he sprints out her door.

Standing in the kitchen alone with the aroma of a great meal for two, Dallas's absence looms large. *I really hope he gets his dream, I do...but am I a bad person because part of me wishes he doesn't so he stays here with me?*

The timer on the stove dings; Baxter and Mimi trot in, wagging their tails. "You two are going to have a feast tonight."

At the end of the unexpected dull and disappointing evening, Jillian lounges cuddled up in her yoga pants with the dozing dogs flipping through cable channels. She zooms past a local news station showing highlights from the night's baseball game, then clicks back to see who won Game Two.

"Got to hand it to the Bishops though, they deserve the landslide victory after totally outplaying the Cougars tonight," the sportscaster accepts the defeat gracefully.

*Thanks Boston, I lost again.* Jillian shuts off the TV. *Dallas would be in his glory right now...and I'd be doing God knows what at his beck and call.* Her mind wanders off to remember the strength of his loving young body, the V-cut lines embossed in his torso, the way he kisses with such tenderness yet at the same time untamed primal lust.

Her cell beeps. She drags her mind out of its erotic center and reaches for the mobile to see who's texted her so late.

*Dallas?* Her mood immediately perks up.

"I won again. Surprise surprise. You ready?"

She is surprised—and thrilled--to hear from him. She types back, "Little hard when you're in Phoenix."

"I'm never a little hard with you in mind :) Do U video chat?"

"I have Crype on my laptop."

"Cool. Tomorrow night @10pm your time. Game 2 pay up Baby."

"OK...10pm"

"Heads up...strip show for me...wear black lace...makes me hot."

*Is he serious?* "Nite Dallas," she writes.

She ruffles up the snoring fur babies. "Time for bed. Tomorrow is going to be a long day."

In her bedroom, Baxter and Mimi jump up on the queen size mattress and settle in while Jillian plods over to her closet. *Do I even own any black lace?*

# FIFTEEN

"You're leaving early today," Josephine says to Jillian with a snoopy edge.

"I have an errand to run," she shoots back with an unintended air of secrecy that only makes Josephine want to know more.

"Just as well, the damned system is slow today," she replies, watching Jillian slide on her coat. "I thought Loverboy was out of town?"

"He is."

"Another rooster in the hen house already?"

"Josie," Jillian presses, "I have an appointment across town at four."

"I'm only busting your buttons. You're acting all mysterious like you've got a hot date."

"Well, I guess I do, kind of."

Thirty minutes later Jillian hops off the Back Bay tram and hoofs it over to trendy upscale Newbury Street. Past the designer chocolate shop and contemporary art gallery, she finds a sleek modern entrance tucked away inside a Colonial-bricked alcove. The frosted door is elegantly etched with the name Libida Lux. She looks around the block to make sure no one she knows sees her before she opens the door and slips inside.

The instant she steps into the couture lingerie and accessories shop, she's a teenager again, unsure of herself in an adult x-rated world. But this is her choice, she reminds herself; she could easily go to any department store for lacy panties, however this time it feels like it requires something more. Meeting Dallas Monroe changed the game. Her video strip debut is the perfect reason to take the plunge into the world of exotic clothes. And after reading all the reviews online, Kat is the expert who will be her perfect guide.

"I'll be right with you," a Euro-styled woman behind the counter says to her as she waits on another customer.

"I have an appointment with Kat for a fitting," a skittish Jillian replies.

"I'll let her know," she says politely then presses a button on the phone with a long red fingernail. "She'll be out in a few minutes, please take a look around."

Jillian meanders over to a wall display of fine lace bras and thongs. Exquisitely beautiful, she admires the intricate delicate patterns and can't help but touch the velvet and feather trim on a pair of elbow-length gloves.

She wanders over to the piece de resistance commanding the corner's attention: a sensual mannequin clad in a revealing leather bodysuit decked out in shiny buckles and silver studs. The striking outfit fascinates her as much as it scares her. Jillian flips over the price tag and nearly has a heart attack. *It's more than my mortgage payment!*

"That would look great on you," a deep husky female voice booms. "Want to try it on?"

Jillian turns to see a woman with a punk rock edge towering over her in stilettos. A severely-cropped quasi-blonde with serious eyeliner, this woman looks like she's earned every torn hole in her black skintight wardrobe.

"No, thanks." Jillian tries not to visibly tremble. "Are you Kat?"

"The one and only. I pulled a few ensembles for you based on our phone conversation but now that I see you, I think I want to show you something else. D cup 34?" she guesses looking Jillian over.

"B 32," Jillian corrects her demurely.

"Don't think so. Let's get you measured, true fit is everything. Grab the changing room on the left, I'll get my tape," Kat directs. Jillian watches the tall assertive woman stomp off in her gravity-defying heels. *She could squash a man to death between those thighs.*

Wired camisoles of French lace and magnificently-crafted bras hang preselected for Jillian in the fitting room. Racier than she'd ever dare wear, she holds them up in front of herself in the mirror.

Kat whooshes the curtain aside. A measuring tape dangles around her neck as she holds up a padded hanger with a sexy black lace outfit. "This is it. This one is for you," Kat says with full-confidence--as if anyone would ever challenge her. Certainly not Jillian who looks at the suspender and halter bra lingerie convinced she could never wear that in front of another living soul.

Kat measures Jillian. "Yep, D 34, I was dead on. You've been wearing the wrong size all this time, honey."

"I had know idea."

"That's why they pay me the big bucks. You've got a great rack, show 'em off. Why stuff 'em down into a smaller cage?" Kat advises then corrects herself, "Unless you're into that." After the hard-edged woman hangs the garment up on a fitting room hook, she stands back to admire it. "Love Italian lace. Try it on, I'll be back in a few minutes to see what you think."

Alone, Jillian runs her fingertips along the small dainty-lace ruffles on the hem of the suspender skirt. She loves it, but wishes she had an ounce of Kat's self-confidence to pull it off. She starts to undress, thinking about Dallas's reaction to her in it.

"How are you doing in there?" Kat's loud voice cuts through the curtain. "Do you need anything? How does it fit?"

Jillian, now encased in this provocative lace lingerie, stands looking at the woman in the mirror, one she's never seen before. And she likes what she sees: her body cloaked in a see-through halter bra, suspenders, and garters. Jillian Miles is a hot vixen.

"Yes, it fits great but I think I need another pair of panties. These have a big tear in them," she calls out.

Kat grows concerned, "Oh? I didn't see that they were damaged. That sucks. Let me see?"

"Sure," Jillian said, inviting her in.

"Wow, you look phenomenal!" Kat's genuine compliment means the world to her. "Turn around."

Jillian complies, feeling herself move differently, with a fluid sass that seems to have appeared out of nowhere.

"I love how this feels on, it makes me feel...powerful...sexy."

"That's the real deal with lingerie: ultimately it's not about how it makes you look, it's how it makes you feel. So where's the rip? I'll kill whoever did that and didn't tell me."

Jillian points to it.

Kat blinks fast, hesitates, unsure if Jillian is serious or joking. "That's not a rip, honey, they're crotchless. You know that, right?"

The Jillian before Dallas Monroe would've died a thousand embarrassed deaths right then and there. But this Jillian doesn't. She starts to laugh. She laughs away her naivete and her prudish upbringing. She laughs away her frigid mother and useless ex-husband. She just laughs. And then so does Kat.

"Good one. I'll have to use that line," Kat says. "Anything else I can help you with today?"

Jillian points down at Kat's red-soled, five-inch heels. "Can you teach me to walk in those?"

# SIXTEEN

After a light dinner and a nap, Jillian gets ready for her online debut with Dallas. She pulls the fine lace lingerie of the Libida Lux bag and snips off the tag. Smack in the middle of taking off her jeans, the phone rings. She hurriedly pushes her denim straight legs to the floor to get across the room before she misses it in case it's Dallas.

Her shoulders sag when she sees the caller ID. *Ugh, What does he want?*

"Greg?"

"Hi Jillian, sorry to bother you. I got a call today from Jonathan. That investment we made with him matures at the end of this month. I totally forgot about it. He wants us to meet with him to discuss where to put the money next."

"Can't we just cash it out?"

"Yes, but that's not smart. It would be better in the long run to keep investing it."

Jillian is annoyed with him always calling the financial shots, especially now after their divorce. "Fine, let's talk to Jonathan about it," she rushes him off the phone, not wanting to discuss it—or even be talking to him—while she's getting ready for Dallas.

"Can you meet tomorrow afternoon?"

"Tomorrow? You know I work," she's pissed at the short notice. *It's always about his convenience.*

"It's the only time I can make it. I can call Jonathan and see if we can meet at five, would that work?"

*I just want to get this over with.* "Let me know," she surrenders with a heavy sigh.

She hangs up and wants to get the Greg energy out of the air. *I refuse to let him taint my evening with Dallas.*

She slips on the brand new pair of stilettos that Kat taught her to walk in and practices prancing around the room. *Small steps. Heel then toe, heel then toe. Walk a straight line. I so got this.* She pauses and hunches over her laptop and scrolls through an online streaming app for some music to put her in the right mood. Sultry electronica saturates the room. *Perfect. Now for some candles and wine. Lots of wine.*

Still in a blouse and panties, she struts her proudly confident stiletto stuff toward the kitchen. But when her yet-to-be-scruffed-up-soles come off the carpeting and hit the slippery linoleum, her feet go flying out from underneath her. *Shit!* Jillian falls and lands flat on her ass. Hearing the loud crash that made the apartment shake, Mimi comes running in to make sure she's okay.

"I'm fine," she reassures the Westie who licks her with a face that questions why her mom is now on the kitchen floor half-naked. Baxter peeks fearfully around the corner. "Nothing broken, just humbled," she pets Mimi. "So not sexy, Jillian," she humorously chastises herself, sliding the shoes off before getting up. *Please dear God don't let me wipe out in front of Dallas tonight... Note to self: stay on the carpet!*

Eventually everything is in place: scented candles lit, wine poured, sexy outfit on underneath her clothes. Anticipation runs neck in neck with her nervousness. She puts her heels back on and dances to the music, trying out some stripping moves. *This is fun. Sexy fun.* While unbuttoning her shirt to the beat of the music, she notices that Mimi and Baxter are watching her every seductive move. *I can't do this in front of you two.* "In the bedroom you guys, go on," she orders and shepherds them into the next room.

Shutting the door behind her, she walks back into the living room, carefully, to hear Crype ring on her laptop. Her gut does a somersault.

*Here we go. Showtime.*

She slips down into the chair and accepts his video call. Dallas's handsome smiling face lights up the whole the screen. *He's so damn cute.*

"Hey Jilly, how goes it?" he says, leaning back in his chair. *He's not wearing a shirt!*

"Hi. Good, thanks. What's going on with Fall Ball?" she takes a sip of wine.

"Love that you're drinking my wine," he wisecracks. "Pretty good so far. I met with a manager and trainer, but looks like I'll have to stick around a little longer than I thought."

"Oh? How long?" she asks, concerned she'll lose any more of what little time she does have left with him.

"Just another day or so. We're waiting for an owner to show up for my tryouts."

"You don't have to worry about Baxter."

"You're sweet, thanks. Where are the gremlins?"

"In the other room."

Dallas's eyes reflect his inner thoughts which have just switched from casual conversation to lusty pursuits. "Only down-side of me staying on is I'll miss Game Three with you tomorrow. I like to be right there with you to collect my winnings."

"Boston will win this one, you'll see."

"Speaking of seeing and collecting...I've been waiting for this all day."

Jillian, empowered by the safe distance that the computer creates between them, finds herself feeling surprisingly bold. "So have I."

"I want to see you move for me," he orders her in his deepest voice.

"Will that turn you on?" She baits him with a strong sensual voice, leaning slowly toward the laptop camera.

"You'll see how it does."

Although the erotic tech music had got her to this place, it doesn't seem to the job anymore. She stands, bending over to give him a little cleavage preview while she searches her streaming music app for something, well, more stripper-friendly. Her long hair and lips are now front and center in a close up shot on the monitor.

"Love that mouth," he purrs. "What are you doing over there?"

"Looking for music," she smiles.

"Don't keep me waiting too long," he protests.

"Relax. Keep your pants on."

"Not wearing any." She explores that image in her mind which makes her body smolder."This works," she says, clicking on a hip-hop tune and then turning the volume way up. Satisfied, she blows the camera a kiss.

"Show me, baby."

She marches away from the table, just far enough in the living room to give him a full view of herself in her hot new sexy shoes. Heavy bass notes slide and slur deep, causing Jillian to dip her hips and sway like a cobra to the booming rhythm. Another woman takes over her body and she completely lets go. Gyrating and shimmying, she lets the song take her wherever it does. Even though she dances to the computer, to Dallas, this has become all about her own entertainment.

She teases the computer, moving closer to it while unbuttoning her shirt in tantalizing slow motion to reveal the sheer black lace halter bra she now prizes. She loves showing it off to him.

Not looking at the screen while she dances, she hears him say "You're so fucking hot." His desire for her propels her to go miles past her old comfort zone. She likes turning him on—and feeling that power she has to do so.

With the song nearing its end, she stops and stands facing him with legs shoulder-width apart with a fierce look in her eyes. She swivels her hips and starts unzipping her jeans, one tooth at a time. She rocks her hips to the beat until the denim drops to the floor, showing off her black panties and suspenders. She turns and shakes her ass at him, lifting up her hair and running her hands through it.

The song hits its last note and the room goes dead quiet— except for Dallas who is yelling out exactly what he wishes he was doing to her right then and there.

Jillian, returning to her old self, turns and walks back to the chair and sits. The look on Dallas's face is priceless to her.

"Holy shit, I never knew you had that in you," he is flabbergasted by her performance.

"Neither did I," Jillian giggles, happy with herself.

"I've never been so hard in my life," he professes. "See what you did to me?"

Dallas shows her and her awkwardness creeps back in just enough to make her slightly uncomfortable. All of this is still new to her. But it's with him, her Dallas, so she goes with it, intrigued to explore yet another sexual frontier.

She watches him tug on himself, lost in his frenzy of ever-growing excitement. His eyelids clamp shut to hold off the force inside him roaring to come out. But he breaks free in the nick of time, staving the lustful demon off for the time being.

"Touch it for me," he urges her. "Please, baby, I need to see it."

She hesitates on doing THAT so...so publicly. But she wants to please him, she wants to try it, so Jillian takes a deep breath then slides her hand down the fine black lace crotchless panties. She closes her eyes to conjure up a little privacy. When she touches the folds of her sex, it's only then she realizes how equally turned on she has become.

"Yeah, like that, baby," he groans before she dips into her hand into her own self-pleasure.

The sexy sounds she hears from Dallas give her the feeling they're doing this together. She rubs and inserts her fingers in her pussy the way she wishes he was doing it for her. Her body rocks uncontrollably on the wooden dining room chair. Dallas's grunts accompany her while waves of heat and ecstasy course through her body until there's no place left to go. Her explosive orgasm nearly knocks her off the seat. She lingers there, reeling from its magnitude, before opening her eyes to witness Dallas, her partner in virtual sex crime, experiencing his own.

They both sit wiped out, happily.

"You always amaze me, gorgeous," he praises her now back in his normal tone.

"I'm glad."

"That was great. I so needed that. But I should get a move on now. Early meeting tomorrow," he says in his usual detached post-sex way.

"What, we're not going to cuddle now?" she busts his chops.

He laughs. "When I get back. Promise."

"Yeah, that's what they all say. Good luck out there. See you when you get back."

# SEVENTEEN

"They're in the conference room down the hall on the right," the legal secretary directs Jillian.

"Thank you," she says heading off to face Greg and the lawyer. *Drum up the mojo, Jillian.*

"Oh, Miss?" the woman calls out, stopping her midway down the corridor. "Love your shoes, Jimmy Choo?"

Jillian is psyched that someone noticed her new insatiable desire for sexy shoes. "On sale," she half-whispers back, as if they were sharing a woman-to-woman secret. Somehow the reminder gave her a stronger sense of herself as she enters the meeting.

"Jillian, nice to see you," the lawyer greets her, rising to his feet.

"Jonathan," she shakes his hand. "Greg," she addresses the ex, who's busy scrutinizing her with a puzzled look.

"You look different," he says at her more than to her. "New hair do?"

"No," she dismisses him and takes her seat.

"Okay, let's get started, shall we?" The lawyer spreads out a stack of papers while Greg is still analyzing his ex-wife. "Everything except this account was reinvested after the divorce. As I mentioned to Greg, with the market the way it is, I strongly suggest reinvesting the funds instead of a cash payout. I'm thinking of this hedge fund," he says handing them some paperwork.

"Looks fine, Jonathan. Go ahead. We'll take your advice."

"Well, hold on, Greg, I need Jillian's approval too."

"Isn't that the money we had set aside for opening my restaurant?" Jillian asks looking at the document with a healthy six-figure amount.

"Yes, but you know we've been all though that. A restaurant isn't a practical idea. It's a ridiculous fantasy. Don't screw with your retirement over some unrealistic pipe dream."

Jonathan clears his throat. "Do you want to talk about this privately and get back to me? You know I charge by the hour."

"Oh I know, I'm sure I paid for that watch you're wearing," Greg sarcastically joshes him. "But I'm sure Jillian will agree."

Jillian doesn't look at Greg, "When do you have to have an answer?"

"Two weeks tops."

Greg loses his cool. "Don't play games, Jillian, just sign off on this and get it over with. It's smart advice."

"I'm not doubting that," she responds trying to keep her composure. Under the table she crosses her open-toed stilettos and asks, "Jonathan, are there any tax issues I should be aware of if I cash out versus rolling over?"

"Yes. I'd talk to your accountant."

"Then I think I should. Hold off on the paperwork until I've talked to him?"

"What has gotten into you?" Greg demands.

*It's more like 'who' has gotten into me, you condescending prick.* "Gentlemen, I'll be in touch."

# EIGHTEEN

Back at the office, working on the report that she didn't finish before going to the lawyer's office, Jillian toggles back and forth from her database screen to Game Three. By the fifth inning the writing is on the wall for Boston. *He's going to win again.*

And he does. St. Louis destroys Boston 12-2.

Not long after the game ends, Jillian calls it a night and gathers up her things to head home. She shuts off her desk light when her cell phone beeps. *Let me guess.*

"3 down, 1 to go! SWEEP! Home tomorrow. Get ready...I've missed that body."

She writes back playfully, "You knew there could be a sweep and you withheld that. Unfair advantage...agreement null and void."

"NO WAY...your ass is mine tomorrow night. And every other part of you."

She's glad that he can't see her smile because she revels in the fact that, as far as she's concerned, they do belong to him. And for as long as they can.

# NINETEEN

With the local and national press still snapping photos after Rep. William Avery Miles III tossed his re-election hat in the Massachusetts political ring, the entire Miles brood file into a posh hotel function room for a post-fundraiser celebration. Hoping to avoid her mother and have some fun at the event, Jillian scans the room for her favorite cousins.

"Jill, over here," Suzanne, her hysterical first cousin, calls her over. Jillian waves back, perking up. *Saved by Susie...at least now the afternoon won't go with out a few good laughs.*

But before she makes a move in her cousin's direction, her mother appears out of nowhere and grabs her by the arm. She turns to see the flawlessly coiffed matriarch standing with a man she's never met, about her age in a Harvard blazer. She knows that look in her mother's eyes. *She's up to something.*

"James, this is my daughter, Jillian."

"Hello, pleasure to meet you," the attractive preppy man says respectfully and shakes her hand.

"James is a speechwriter. He's signed on to your father's campaign and we're fortunate to have him aboard. I told him you'd love to fill him in on our family history."

Jillian sees where this is leading and doesn't want to go. "Well Lauren would probably be better at that than I would."

Icy steel daggers from her mother's eyes slice her in two. "She's just being modest, James. Jillian has always been shy. I've saved a pair of seats for you at the table over there, so you can talk without the family babble getting in your way."

Jillian's insides clench tight. James, however, has no problem exploiting this opportunity with the Congressman's lovely daughter.

"That would be delightful, Mrs. Miles. Thank you. Jillian, if you'll excuse me while I check my messages, I'll meet you at the table in a minute," he articulates with boarding school manners and heads out into the hall for Wi-Fi.

"Mom," Jillian whines.

"Don't you "Mom" me. He's from a good family."

"There's more to it than that, you know."

"Jillian Miles, I've held my tongue for five long years. It's bad enough your father is running his campaign on family values with a divorced daughter. A single divorcee is even worse. James is a prime catch; if you can't find a good husband on your own, then I will find one for you."

Over her mother's shoulder, Jillian sees James walking back into the bustling room of local press and loyal voters. She feels suffocated and cornered. Her mind wanders to Dallas and her impending date. *I gotta get out of here.*

When James rejoins them, she tells them both, "I'm not feeling well all of a sudden, I'm sorry, I think I should go home." She rubs her stomach while shielding her gaze from her mother's fury. Without wasting a beat, Jillian politely apologizes to James, "It was nice to meet you. Another time perhaps?"

"I hope so," he says, disappointed.

Not waiting for another word from either of them, Jillian immediately takes off. Pushing her way through the crowd and stuffy rooms, she needs desperately to get outside for some fresh air.

Every mile she drives between her and the fundraiser makes her calmer and freer. By the time she gets home, she's back to her happy self and thinking about nothing except her big date that night.

Dallas's red jeep is impossible to miss when Jillian pulls into her apartment parking lot. *He's back.* A wry smile creeps across her face as she unbuckles her seat belt. There is nothing she wants more than to spend a leisurely torrid night at home alone with him, just her and Dallas. The very thought of him naked and touching her puts an extra swing in her hips as she sashays into her side of the building.

"Mimi, I'm home," she calls out, walking through the door. As soon as she steps inside, her eyes are immediately drawn to her dining room table which is covered with stuff, none of which she put there. *What the hell is all that?*

Her best white silk blouse with pearl buttons hangs neatly pressed on its hanger on the back of a dining chair. Her black microfiber mini skirt is splayed out on the table next to her latest pair of stilettos. The only thing she doesn't recognize is the shopping gift bag in the center of it all.

She peers into the bag and pokes through its pink and silver tissue. *Pretty paper.* She pulls out a a pair of red and black lace G-string panties that had fallen out of their wrapping. *He didn't.* She rifles the contents for more and unwraps its counterpart: a black demi bra that you might as well be wearing nothing. *Oh my God.* The only thing left in the bag is an envelope with her name on it.

With her heart palpitations escalating, she takes out the note,

St. Louis pay up time :) Get dressed and be ready for
me at 8pm tonight.
–D

Jillian's face flushes, more from anticipation of what's to come
than her default go-to embarrassment in the past. She picks up
the bra and panties and checks their sizes. Perfect. "Was he in
here going through my bureau, Mimi?" she asks the little dog
who cocks her head trying to translate. "Some protector you
are!" she kids, turned on by the image playing in her head of
him sneaking in to carry out his kinky reconnaissance mission.
"Let's see how these fit."

Hours pass until it's nearly Dallas date time. Jillian, outfitted
in her assigned sexiness, flits about her apartment doing mindless
chores while the clock ticks as slow as molasses. She loves that the
thong he bought her feels tight against her crotch; it makes her
continuously horny as she moves. Then again, everything about
Dallas Monroe keeps her constantly aroused.

She checks the clock for the umpteenth time.

7:59. *Any second now, he'll be here. I can't wait to see him!*
Jillian rushes over to the mirror to check her hair and lipstick
one last time.

8:06. *Where is he?* She busies herself, unsuccessfully, to try
to keep her mind off the clock.

8:12. Her excitement is starting to tank. *It's not like him to
be this late.*

The minutes seem eternal until finally her cell phone beeps a
text message at sixteen past. *Oh please don't tell me he's not coming.*
She grabs the phone with worry.

"Put your coat on and meet me outside. I'm waiting for you," his message says.

She types back, "Be right down."

*What is he up to?* She throws on a long wool shawl to ward off the nippy night air and grabs her keys. "Don't wait up," she tells Mimi and flies down the stairs.

Idling right outside her door at the curb is the red Cherokee; its empty passenger seat right there in front of her waiting for her to get in. "Hey, gorgeous," he utters warmly from the driver's seat.

Her first thought is how great it is to see him. A quick second thought, however, is how the hell is she going to climb up and into the jeep with her high heels?

"Welcome back," she says, stalling until she formulates a game plan. He catches on to her dilemma though and hops out of the running 4x4 to aid his damsel in distress. He strolls around the jeep and like nothing sweeps her up and off her gold heels then slides her inside onto the passenger seat. Unexpected chivalry, unforeseen new level of attraction. "Thanks," she gleams.

"Not a problem," he says all manly. She watches him through the windshield as he swaggers around the hood and hops back in behind the wheel. "You look awesome," he raves, and gives her a kiss that she can feel all the way down into her toes. "Missed those lips," he murmurs before shifting gear. "Among other things."

"Where are we going?" she asks playfully as he drives out of the apartment complex.

"You'll find out soon enough." Dallas reaches down between her legs to grab something from under the seat. He caresses her smooth bare calf with a velveteen pouch he's pulled out from under her before tossing it into her lap. "Here, put this on."

"What is this?"

"Just put it on."

Jillian removes a black eye mask from the bag and yanks on its elastic band. "Seriously?"

"Trust me."

She pulls the mask over her head and adjusts it over her eyes. "I can't see a thing."

"Good. And no peeking."

"Dallas, where are you taking me?" she demands eagerly.

He doesn't answer. The jeep twists and turns down seemingly endless streets. The ongoing silence heightens when the Cherokee stops, she assumes, at a red light. The surprise motion of Dallas placing his hand on her inner thigh makes the muscles in her leg involuntarily shudder—even more so when he slowly runs it up towards her crotch. "You don't know how much I've wanted you since we Cryped." Her hips squirm in the bucket seat and she grabs her chest, suspecting he's leering at every part of her and getting turned on just as much as she is. When someone behind them beeps their horn, he lets go of her to shift gear; they continue driving onward to wherever.

After a good twenty minutes on the road by her estimation, they stop. He cuts the engine and pulls the keys out of the ignition. "We're here," he announces and removes the mask for her.

She squints to regain her full sight. Looking at the sign and colored lights she blinks to make sure what she's seeing is for real. The Fuzzy Cherry is no illusion and neither is the banner above the door that reads "Amateur Night Tonight".

She panics. "I can't go in there."

"Sure you can. It'll be fun."

"Dallas, I can't," she squeals, her sexual self-confidence reverting way back to before she met him.

"It's just a bar, really. Why not?"

"Why not? Someone might see me."

"That's the whole point."

"Dallas," she freaks. "I only want to be with you like this."

"I know. And believe me, I love every ounce of that. But when I'm gone, then what? We gotta reach for new horizons while we can."

She doesn't want the reminder that she's losing him, although she knows he's got a point.

"Couples do this all the time to jazz up their sex lives. It'll be a blast...and really fucking hot to see you up on stage. I'm right there with you all the way. You'll be great. What's the worst thing that can happen?"

"On stage?" she shrieks.

"You're a natural. Witnessed it myself. Admit that it turned you on when you stripped for me."

"But that was different."

"Nah. That was just the dress rehearsal...or undress rehearsal I should say. I bet anything you'll be into this way more than you ever imagined."

"I'll die of embarrassment."

"If you haven't by now, doubt you ever will."

*True.* Jillian sits still and stares out the window.

"If you're really dead set against it, I'll take you home. It's your call, Jilly," he says kindly.

She knows he wouldn't push her to do something she really didn't want to do. They sit for awhile without a word between them, watching men wander in and out of The Fuzzy Cherry. *Well, I am curious...and if I'm ever going to venture into place like this, I'd rather do it with Dallas...please don't let anyone I know be in there.* "I'm going to need a stiff drink. Or three," she insists.

Dallas opens the club door for her and instantly the smell of cheap fruity perfume and sweat bombards her as she steps inside. The thump thump thump of the woofer vibrates the floor beneath her as strobe lights circle and spin up and down over a runway stage circled by men in padded club chairs being served by beautiful women in push-up bustiers and lace. Her heart rhythm entrains to the beat, her eyes adjust to a very unfamiliar scene. *If I just keep my attention on Dallas everything will be alright.*

"Over there," Dallas says, leading them to a small table at the side of the glossy-floored stage full of scantily dressed dancers working it for greenbacks. Men gawk at Jillian as she passes; she ignores their stares and looks down as she walks by. *This has to be most nasty and outdated carpeting I've ever seen.*

Once seated, she feels some sense of safety but keeps her shawl on for extra protection. Jillian dares to take her first real look around the joint: tables overflow with empty bottles and plastic cups, women slithering up and down metal poles on stage under red and purple neon lights. And of course there's the half-naked women serving drinks to college guys and a few business men in suits who hand them cash to chat with them a little longer. There's money exchanging hands—or stuffed in racy clothing--everywhere.

"What do you think?" Dallas leans in and asks her.

"Pretty much what I thought it would be," Jillian answers, still unsure about the whole thing.

"Let's get you a drink," he calls over a waitress from behind Jillian.

Unbeknownst to Jilly, the striking red-lipsticked woman with jet black hair comes toward them with her tray and a big attitude. Her skintight tube dress can barely contain her in-your-face fake boobs. She slinks around the table to take their order.

"Jillian?" the exotic dancer-turned-waitress gasps.

"Kiki?" Jillian goes white and feels like she's going to throw up.

"You two know each other?" Dallas is surprised yet amused in a way only a guy could be.

"My old man used to be her old man," Kiki clues him in, then studies the young Dallas Monroe before giving Jillian a dirty smile. "Nice shawl," she takes a barely disguised dig at her predecessor, "What'll it be?"

"Guinness for me," Dallas orders, eyeballing Kiki's enormous bouncy rack.

"Dirty Martini. Make it a double," Jillian says emphatically, undoing her woolen wrap. *Bitch.* The last thing she wants is to be out-sexed by Kiki in front of Dallas—been there done that with Greg. A sense of competition eclipses her timidness.

"Comin' right up," Kiki responds with a shit-eating grin and walks off.

A middle-aged man walks onto the stage with a microphone. "And now, the one and only, the infamous Fantasia!"

Men whistle and holler while the deejay turns the volume way up and spins a raunchy hypnotic hip-hop tune. Impossible now to hear anyone talk, the audience turns their eyes to the stage waiting for the featured dancer. Jillian, transfixed, watches a statuesque self-assured female prance her curvaceous goods down the runway like she has the world on a choke hold leash. *Damn.*

Seemingly fearless, the voluptuous woman in thin 6-inch heels strikes a dominant pose—legs apart and hands on her silver G-stringed hips at the edge of the stage as she surveys the men, clearly her regulars, who worship her with dollar bills and catcalls begging her to proceed. Once satisfied with their adulation, she pivots with an elegant flair, swaying her big booty to and fro before bending down ever so slowly to shake her juicy junk in their face. The crowd goes wild when she wiggles each cheek one at a time.

*She owns these guys.* Jillian, mesmerized, takes mental notes throughout the strip performance which stays high sensual voltage up until the very last note of the song when the dancer swings her badass topless self around and around the shiny steel pole. Men hurl a cloud of money onto the foot of the runway.

Fascinated, she watches the appreciative stripper collect her cash. *Wow, she seriously rocked that...okay sure she has a great figure and moves really well, but what it really all boils down to, what these guys were just eating up and hungering for more isn't her body, it's that confidence that oozes out of her. Just look at her, even now she's got it streaming out of her pores. Her cocky, self-loving attitude is everything.*

Kiki reappears with their order and Dallas hands her a wad of five and ten dollar bills.

"How much are these drinks?" Jillian asks taking the martini glass.

"You're not sucking down lemonade at Chucky Cheese, honey." She gives Jillian a snotty look which Jillian gives right back to her before she leaves to serve the table nearby.

The emcee walks back on stage after the exotic dancer has disappeared. "Good evening, welcome to Amateur Night at The Fuzzy Cherry. All of the ladies here in the club who wish to participate in tonight's contest please head over to the DJ booth and sign up within the next ten minutes, if you haven't already. We'll be starting the competition at 10pm. Thank you and good luck."

Dallas turns to Jillian. "So? What do you think?"

Jillian chews on her bottom lip, bluffing, "I think...," she utters meekly then looks him in the eye, "I'm going to win this." She grins and twirls a section of her ashen long hair.

"Yeah you are!" he gives her a high five and a kiss. Dallas is over the moon.

"Let me go see the deejay before it's too late."

Three tipsy sorority sisters giggle as they leave the DJ booth and pass Jillian going in.

"Hi, I'd like to sign up for the contest, please," Jillian says politely.

DJ RunDaze checks her out head to toe. "I'd like you to sign up too. Here ya go." He hands Jillian a questionnaire and release form.

"Thanks," she replies and fills it out while he watches her.

"First time?"

"Yes," she answers and hands him the completed paperwork.

"Thought so," he pauses to look at her name. "Sweetheart, is Jillian Miles your real name?"

"Yes, do you need my ID?"

He laughs, enamored by her innocence. "No, no. But you should use a stage name or every horny dude in this place will be looking you up on his smartphone."

"Oh, God. Thanks. That wouldn't be a good thing."

"Nah, not so much."

Jillian racks her brain trying to come up with a name. *Diamond? Bambi? Pussy Willow?* She can't help but laugh at what she's doing—and imagining the scandal that she would cause if the media found out that Congressman Miles's daughter is stripping at The Fuzzy Cherry. *Wait, that's it.* She scribbles down the name and hands it to the DJ.

"Scandal? That's hot. Alright now some basics you should be aware of when performing: No rubbing your tits or pussy on stage. And hands off the customers. Keep it sexy but clean if you get my drift."

"That won't be a problem," Jillian dismisses quickly.

"You come up on stage when Eddy calls your name and you leave when you're done. No hogging time from the next girl. Be courteous, which something tells me you are."

"Okay, got it," she replies, "Thanks." She hightails it out of there before she changes her mind when he stops her.

"Yo! Wait up, what's your music?"

"What?"

"Your song. What do you want to dance to?"

Jillian's mind is a blank and she throws up her hands.

"Here, take a look at this list." DJ RunDaze grabs a CD with his face on the cover off the mixing board and flips it over.

She can't think straight so just points to one randomly.

"Gotchya. Kill it out there, Scandal," he winks.

Back at the table, she feeds off Dallas's excited buzz and anticipation. Together they watch the first contestant and critique her like they're judges on American Stripper Idol. The second girl gets a good response from the audience but Dallas downplays her, "You're so much better than her." She takes his feedback to heart.

The third girl, a busty drunken college girl whose loud and obnoxious sorority sisters are cheering her on, wanders up on stage when her name, Roxie Rockets, is called. DJ RunDaze spins a heavy metal tune with a sleazy guitar riff. With all eyes on her and the song blaring, Roxie stands frozen with stage fright. A tense vibe fills the strip club and pity for this girl who obviously got talked into something she couldn't handle. Eddy comes back on stage, cues the deejay to cut the song, and escorts the young lady off stage.

"Poor kid. I hope that doesn't happen to me," Jillian recoils a bit.

"Just forget who's watching. Remember who you're doing it for."

"You?" she teases him.

"You. And yeah, okay me. If you get scared, just look at me. We're a team."

Eddy returns to the stage. "Now for our last contestant of the evening, Gentlemen, please get it up for Scandal Monroe."

Dallas laughs hard. "Perfect!" He cheers her on with a squeeze of her knee, "Go for it, baby."

When Jillian rises to her feet, she spots Kiki who sends her a 'You? You've got to be joking' look. She digs down deep to channel the strong, confident, fuck you-attitude she learned from Kat and the mesmerizing Fantasia. *I AM Scandal Monroe.* She struts up on stage with a vengeance.

DJ Rundaze gives her a thumbs up as Prince's voice permeates the club and a funky bass line which kicks in. Jillian--that is Scandal--puts a hand on her hip and prowls the perimeter of the stage with a you-wish-you-could-fuck-this stride, inspecting every leering face in the crowd with unrelenting power and charisma. Her eyes lock with Kiki causing Jillian to pause, cock her hip out, and glare a hole right through the husband-stealing bitch.

When she hears Dallas scream her name, she pivots on her high heel with conviction then swishes her black mini skirt ass over to dance directly to him. Her hips undulate a continuous slow figure eight to the melody, all the while unzipping and sliding the microfiber garment down her smooth thighs until it lands around her stilettos. Dallas goes over to the side of the stage and stuffs a dollar bill in her G-string. " You own this!" he shouts up to her. She winks at him before other men follow suit with their cash tips.

Turning her back to the frothing male audience, she struts off to the center of the stage, keeping with the beat of the the song, all the while unbuttoning her blouse with fiery determination. She plays with the men by peering back over her shoulder and holding out the open left shirt front like a flap; then the right. When the song breaks into its chorus, she whips off the silk blouse and dramatically tosses it onto the floor. In total control, she faces forward, giving them all a sight to behold. The cheers are deafening.

Now with testosterone popping in every corner of the night-club, Jillian gyrates and whips her long loose hair around in hell-bent circles. She grabs onto the stripper pole, arching her back into an impressive back bend that even she didn't know she could do. *Thank you, yoga.* She wraps her stiletto-ed leg around the metallic shaft and spins, reaching her arm up high over head before letting go and slinking her backside down against the pole until she's in a full squat. With a hand on each knee, she opens and closes her thighs erotically to the rhythm of Prince's melody.

Dallas, awestruck and proud, can't believe she's capable of this.

Dropping her palms to the floor, Jillian crawls like a sensual jaguar toward the front of the stage, her cleavage leading the way. In her peripheral vision she sees money being tossed at her all along the side of the runway. She stops, sits up on her knees shoulder-width apart, closes her eyes, and mounts and humps an imaginary lover on the floor. Amid admiring hoots and whistles, she runs her fingers through her hair as she writhes. Her hands slide down across her chest and along her arms until she reaches behind and unhooks her demi bra. She hangs her body forward to release her breasts from the garment, pulling down one tempting strap at a time. The club goes wild.

Now fully topless, she sways her way up to standing to take one last overview of her erotic subjects who rush the stage, showering their sexy queen with dollars just as the song ends. The clapping and whistling continue on well after she's finished.

Eddy takes the stage while she gathers up her loot—and clothing--from the stage. "Well, Gentlemen, I believe the winner tonight is unanimous. Scandal Monroe! Let's give her one more hand," he says and the men do enthusiastically. He murmurs off-mike to Jillian, "Meet me in the DJ both for your prize money."

Another song comes on and the lights dim back down. The club gets back to its regular groove when dancers take their posts around The Fuzzy Cherry.

"You killed it out there," DJ RunDaze raves to Jillian when she walks into the sound booth.

"Thank you," she says proudly and still on a high from it all. Not to mention turned on.

Eddy enters and takes out a pile of bills from his pocket. "Here ya go, five hundred. Well earned, well deserved." She takes it with a smile. "Are you looking for work? I'd give you a feature spot on weekends," he puts on full-court pressure.

"I appreciate it, but I already have a job."

"Dancing?" he fishes.

"Database engineer," she smirks.

"Pfff. Here, take my card in case you change your mind and want to make some real cash."

She takes it to be polite and heads out to find Dallas. *Time to celebrate.*

Bounding out of the Cherry with Dallas, the cold fresh air feels good on her sweat-soaked skin. Laughing, they run quickly to the jeep hand-in-hand.

"HO-LY SHIT, you were fucking amazing in there," he praises her with utmost sense of awe in his voice when he opens the Cherokee door for her.

She slips off her heels and climbs in like a tomboy. "It was fun, really fun," she confesses, all giddy. "And it really turned me on," she says breathy.

"You think YOU got turned on?" he overstates and shuts her door.

As soon as he gets in his seat, he immediately leans over and kisses her hard. His hand cups her round breast while French kissing her as deeply as she can take; she reaches over and pulls up his shirt and unbuttons his jeans. His bulge grows fast with her action.

"I want you right now," he says hungrily, knowing he can't stop.

The stripping has made her more aroused than she could fathom. "Fuck me right here," she demands.

Dallas can barely contain himself. He tries to take her panties off but the stick shift keeps getting in the way. "Wait, let me put the seat down so we have some room."

"No need," Jillian answers and pushes him back over to his own side. "Push the seat back a little." When he does, she removes her G-string, nimbly climbs over and straddles him. It's a tight squeeze between Dallas's torso and the steering wheel, but it somehow adds to the excitement.

With her knees firmly planted on either side of his muscular legs, she rubs her crotch up and down over his protruding denim bulge. With the close quarters, however, it's not easy to release him from his jeans. She grabs onto the roll bar and pulls herself up and off him just enough for him to set his rock hard cock free. She slides gently right down on it, making him groan with pleasure. She rides him with reckless abandon, yanking on his hair as he devours her neck. They never notice how the heat from their passionate bodies and hot breath completely fog up all the windows.

Her bucking ass accidentally beeps the horn, but they don't stop. They can't.

"I'm close," he pants.

But she's already beat him there and reeling from the waves of orgasm crashing through her body. He joins her soon after and together they wash ashore back onto dry land.

Sweaty isn't the word for it. Her wet hair clings to her face and the jeep feels like a terrarium. Beads of heavy perspiration roll down the side of Dallas's face, prompting him to open the window for some much needed air. Jillian, with her legs absolutely useless at this point, manages to lift herself off Dallas and plop herself back into her own seat to recoup.

After awhile the two lovers glide back into a calm state. "Wow. That was one hell of a night," he swears and turns on the engine.

"I loved it," she confesses without a hint of remorse as they start driving home.

"Too bad Boston is going to get swept next game and the series will end, we're just hitting our prime."

"I've told you, never ever underestimate Boston."

The Cherokee pulls into the apartment complex and he pulls up to her door. She's sleepy but deliriously happy with her evening and being in his company.

"Dallas, stay with me tonight."

He shys away from her offer. "I gotta get some sleep. You should too." He taps her affectionately on the leg.

She's disappointed but unfortunately used to the drill.

"Game Four is tomorrow afternoon but I'll be out of town with Uncle Jack for most of the day. I'll let you know when I'm back...and what I want for my championship trophy."

"Yeah, yeah. Goodnight Dallas," she says kissing him one last time. "And thanks for tonight. I'll never forget it."

"Neither will I. You're incredible, Jillian Miles. Glad you're starting to see that for yourself. Now get some sleep."

Jillian climbs out of the Cherokee, a woman remarkably unlike the one who got in only hours before. Carrying her stilettos, piles of cash, and the strip club owner's card, she looks like a hot slutty mess limping barefoot to her door. *So this is the Walk of Shame...I've never been prouder.*

# TWENTY

"I was starting to think we were going to have send out a search party," Jillian's older sister complains, moving her food around her plate.

"I know, I know, I've just been really busy. What's wrong with your meal?"

"I don't think they cooked it enough, I think I should send it back." She shrivels up her nose and puts her fork down.

Jillian rolls her eyes. *She sends everything back, every time.* Jilly tastes her difficult sibling's roast beef. "It's fine, Lauren. Pretty good, too."

Lauren crosses her arms, careful not to wrinkle her designer sleeves in protest. "When the waiter comes back I'm going to ask him to take it back to the kitchen."

"And you wonder why I don't accept your dinner invitations?" Jillian jokes, sipping her sparkling wine.

"Is that the reason you've been avoiding me?" she probes, a bit hurt.

"No, I haven't been avoiding you. I've been seeing someone," Jillian spills the beans with a smile.

Her elder sister is pleased. "Well, it's about time. Mom will be so relieved that you're finally bringing a date to Thanksgiving next month."

The reality that Dallas will be gone by then kicks her in the gut. "I won't be bringing him to Thanksgiving."

"Why not?" As expected, the interrogation begins.

"He's only here for two more weeks. He travels a lot for work."

"What kind of business is he in? Real estate? Stock broker? Did you hear Melissa Talbot just got engaged to Thomas Albright? He's now a full private equity partner at Reilly & McCann."

She loves bursting her prissy sister's snobby bubble, "He plays baseball. Minor League. I think he's pretty good."

Lauren stares at her, clutches at her throat, speechless. Her face is riddled with disdain.

The waiter comes to their table with a glass of wine for Jillian. "Miss, the gentleman over there sends this with his compliments." He points and places it down on the table for Jillian who scans the bar. A decent looking man in a nice suit raises his glass to her in a toast. She smiles uncomfortably and turns away.

"Who's he?" Lauren demands. Jillian shrugs.

The waiter fills in the pieces. "The gentleman said to tell you he met you last night at Eddy's. Is there anything else I can get for either of you?"

Jillian's back straightens up with mild shock. *He recognizes me?* She looks concerned as she rubs behind her ear, recalling her dance moves as Scandal. "No, thank you," she says to the waiter who leaves them.

"Who's Eddy? The baseball player?"

"No."

"Jillian, who are all these strange men?" Lauren is now in full-on detective mode.

Jillian wants to shock her sister but holds back from going there. "I thought you were sending the beef back?"

"I'm not hungry anymore. Who is Eddy?"

Before Jillian can respond, the man from the bar approaches their table.

"Good evening, what a coincidence running into you again tonight. My luck."

"I'm sorry, I don't think I know you," Jillian tries to give him the brush off.

"Yes, you were at Eddy's last night, weren't you? I never forget a beautiful face."

Lauren sizes him up and his net worth and likes what she sees. Jillian finds the energy of the man's attention just plain wrong.

"No, I'm sorry. You must be mistaking me for someone else."

"I'm sure it was you. I was wondering if you'd like to join me for dinner tomorrow night at the Ritz?"

"Yes she would," Lauren answers powerfully, determined to play matchmaker between her little sister and a big wallet.

Jillian kicks her under the table.

"I'm involved with someone, I'm sorry. Thank you for the drink."

"My loss. I hope we'll see you at Eddy's very soon," he says and leaves.

Jillian is relieved. "What a creep."

"What is wrong with you? A custom suit is not a creep, dating a forty-year old guy wearing a baseball uniform is what's creepy."

Miffed, she sets the record straight, "Dallas is thirty-three, or so. "

"Very funny."

"It's true. And he's gorgeous," she rubs it in and takes a sip of the wine meant for Scandal.

Lauren throws her hands up, confused. "This is all too much. Way too much. First just tell me who Eddy is and why you were with him last night," she demands in her big sister authoritative voice as if she is still eleven years old.

Jillian clicks her fingernail against the crystal stem of wine glass, pensive. *There's nothing to be ashamed about.*

"Eddy owns The Fuzzy Cherry."

It goes right over her Bridge champion sister's head.

"You know, the strip club on Lagrange Street? I went there last night with Dallas."

All the color drains out of Lauren's face. "The Miles don't go to those tawdry places."

"This Miles did. And surprisingly it wasn't so tawdry, more like a casino badly in need of an update."

Aghast, Lauren's skin crawls at even trying to imagine what it looks like inside. "JILLIAN! What on Earth were you doing in there?"

Jillian can't hold back her smile or the truth, "Dancing in Amateur Night, actually. And I won. Made almost a thousand dollars in five minutes. Not bad for a rookie."

Lauren shakes her head a few times to make all this register. She studies her sister desperately for some rational explanation. "Level with me, Sis, are you on drugs? We'll get you into rehab. A nice one, far away so nobody finds out."

Jillian laughs. "No, Lauren. It was fun. A lot of fun. I've never felt so alive."

"Dancing for men is degrading to women."

"I didn't dance for their pleasure, I danced for my own. It was empowering."

Lauren can't contain her anger any longer. "Do you know what would happen to Dad if the media got wind of this? Didn't you even consider the shame you could bring on the family traipsing into a place like that?"

Jillian loses her cool. "I am SO tired of tying my sexuality to what other people think, especially my uptight family who has pretended all my life that sex doesn't exist. Well, Lauren, it does. Human beings have sex. Women have sex and we love it. It's the twenty-first century, for Christ's sake. Get over it already."

Lauren is red in the face. She rises, grabs her purse and coat, and walks out of the restaurant without ever responding.

Jillian remains at the table, shaking a little from the confrontation but also from a major release. She sips her cocktail. A sense of pride overcomes her; she's taken control of her own sensuality after all these years. And it feels immensely liberating.

The waiter pushes a mouth-watering dessert cart next to her table. "May I tempt you with something sweet?"

*Why not?* "Ooh, is that Tiramisu?" He nods and places the fancy china with the decadent cake in front of her. "Thank you."

"Anything else? Coffee? Tea?"

"Espresso please. And by chance, do you know who won the game tonight?"

"Boston, thank heavens," he informs her then takes leave of the table.

*Finally! It's about time I won...even more reason to celebrate. What do I want...how do I want Dallas? Let me count the ways....* Jillian lets a bite of Tiramisu melt in her mouth as she considers several sexy scenarios.

With Lauren no longer blocking her view, Jillian's eyes roam the dining room as she enjoys her Italian dessert and coffee. She spies on a young couple in their late twenties enjoying their dinner date in the corner. *Look at them, they have 'new love' written all over them. She looks so pretty and he's practically glowing when he looks at her. I bet it's their first, maybe second date. How romantic.*

She finishes her espresso and waits for the check. She keeps tabs on the young couple who are now holding hands across the table. *I'd give anything to have a date like that with Dallas.* The young man kisses her hand sweetly and Jillian's heartstrings vibrate with happiness for them and a little jealousy. *That's what I want I want as my win.*

Later at home her phone beeps a text message. "Hey Jilly. Running late so staying overnight. Please get Baxter til tomorrow?"

She replies, "Hi D. Of course."

He responds, "Thx. Should be back by 5."

Jillian answers, "Boston won :)... I have plans for you tomorrow night."

Dallas writes, "I'm all yours, Scandal. See you then."

Jillian looks over at Mimi who rests her head on a sofa pillow. "Let's go get your boyfriend."

Baxter is thrilled to have company. The two dogs chase each other around Dallas's apartment while Jillian takes the opportunity to snoop. *The place feels really empty without him here. I can't imagine how life is going to be after he's gone.* She wanders into the bedroom which has only stacks of storage boxes, most of which have never been opened.

She peers sneakily into an open cardboard carton that has a baseball championship trophy sticking out of it. There's usual guy stuff but then she detects the corner of a small picture frame underneath some books near the bottom of the box. She pulls it out and wipes off the dust. She smiles at the photo of a young Dallas Monroe in his junior varsity baseball uniform with a woman hugging him with lots of love and pride shining in her eyes. *So cute! That's got to be his mom. Oh, poor Dallas. Her death must have been so traumatic for him...and I don't think he's ever really gotten past it.* She gives the boy a sympathetic glance then reburies it.

Jillian walks back into the main room and sits down on the futon mattress. *Amazing how different I am since the first time I sat here. I want this to last forever...but it's not.* Her eyes mist up, looking around. *In a blink we'll be a memory. Josephine is right, I let myself get super attached, but how could I not? I should start pulling back, like Dallas does, no more hoping to make this more than what it is. I can't love him...so tomorrow night will be the night to remember. I'll make it the perfect dream so I can replay it in my mind over and over after...he's gone.* A tear rolls down her face.

Mimi and Baxter scamper onto the futon and look up at her with goofy dog grins. They make her laugh. "Okay, time to go."

# TWENTY-ONE

"Hi Josephine, I'm not coming in today, taking a personal day."

"Okay. Everything alright?"

"Yeah, yeah, I just decided I need a "Me Day". Have some errands to run. There's nothing important that you need me for is there?"

"It'll be tough, but I think we can survive without you," she teases. "Is Loverboy part of this "Me Day"?"

"Today is all about Loverboy," she answers happily.

"Love it. Don't do anything I wouldn't do," Josephine kids her.

"That doesn't leave me much," she jokes. "See you tomorrow. Thanks."

She ends her call with Josephine and dials the next name on her mental list.

"Good morning, Winston Salon and Day Spa, may I help you?"

"Yes, I'd like to make an appointment for this afternoon."

"Certainly. Which services are you looking for? Facial? Hair? Nails? Massage?"

"All of them."

After treating herself to her favorite lunch in Harvard Square, Jillian heads over to the city's upscale shopping mall to do some serious damage to her bank account. Never really one to splurge on expensive clothes, this occasion is something altogether different: the hunt is on for the perfect dress for tonight's date with Dallas.

Every big designer has a shop here. Jillian waltzes up and down one side of the luxury mall, window shopping until the right outfit catches her eye. *It has to be feminine yet alluring. Sexy but classy.* She crosses the large open space to peruse the other side's stores. *There it is.* Excited, she buzzes and the doorman lets her in.

Hours later at the spa, feeling relaxed from her lavender Swedish massage and facial, Jillian has a makeup artist and hair stylist give her a polished look to match the dress and shoes she bought. While still in the salon chair, and with Josef fussing over the finishing touches of her locks, she texts Dallas, "Our reservation for dinner tonight is @ 7pm @ Hotel Emerson. Suit and tie required."

"You look divine," Josef holds up a hand mirror so she can see the back of her head. "A true goddess."

"You're genius, Josef."

"Honey, I'd kiss myself if I could," he agrees wholeheartedly.

# TWENTY-TWO

In the darkness of the Autumn night, Jillian's moment in the sun begins.

At the curb, the doorman opens the cab door for Jillian who steps out in full elegance.

"Good evening, Miss."

"Thank you," she says adjusting her fringed pashmina. She saunters under the red bricked portico of Hotel Emerson, one of Boston's finest.

The lobby is flush with old New England sophistication. The immaculately dressed concierge approaches her, "May I help you?"

"I'm meeting someone," she replies looking around. "Well, maybe he's already at the Long Bar. But thank you." The concierge extends his gloved hand toward its entrance.

Inside the five star restaurant, the buzz of the dinner crowd enjoying rich meals and cocktails in the main dining room spills out into the lounge. Jillian peeks in but sees no trace of him. *Where is he?*

Back in the lounge, she finally spots the back of Dallas who sits at the bar talking to the bartender.

Strolling toward them, the barkeep subtly checks her out and gives Dallas a slight chin nod to take a look. Dallas turns casually to see the hottie who's got the bartender's boxers all in a twist.

The crystals scattered across her champagne silk dress sparkle in the ambient lighting as she walks toward the men. Her soft updo highlights the feminine lines of her beautiful face, her strappy heels showcase her shapely legs. In every sense, she is stunning.

Dallas looks bowled over by her soft radiant beauty; Jillian relishes his continuous stare—and that he's love struck by her sophisticated womanly appearance. *Score. Couldn't have asked for a better reaction.*

"What a honey," the bartender confides over the bar to Dallas who is too entranced by her to answer him.

Jillian reaches the bar and places her hand on Dallas's leg. "Waiting long?"

The bartender is shocked. "She's with you?"

"Better believe it," he says, trying to get in control of himself--and his puppy dog gaze.

Dallas hops off the stool and kisses Jillian carefully on the cheek, as if he were afraid he'd break a precious china doll.

"Look at you in a suit and tie! I knew you'd be handsome," she compliments him playfully and lightly brushes her hand over his.

"Thanks," he answers, all of a sudden a bit off his game. *Wait, is he blushing?*

"You have a real nice night," the bartender says to them, giving Dallas an atta-boy wink after he squares up the bill.

"Thanks, man." Dallas says.

"Nice place, huh?" she asks, proud of her choice.

"I'll say. Didn't think I'd ever be in a bar that didn't have a TV," he jokes.

He nervously adjusts his cuffs before he offers her his arm to escort her toward the main dining room.

"You look absolutely beautiful, Jilly," he says. She flashes him a glowing affectionate smile.

"Thank you," she replies.

As they pass by, random diners take notice of the handsome couple, offering up glances of admiration.

At their cozy white linen draped table tucked away in the back, he holds out the chair for her. She loves how he's stepped up his gentleman's manners. Once seated, Jillian and Dallas explore the Italian cuisine menu.

"I don't even know what half this stuff is," he makes fun of himself, reading the list.

"The chef here is famous for her Sicilian recipes. I love her sauces with seafood. Maybe I'll try the tomato- braised octopus," she says more to herself than to him. She peers over at a puzzled Dallas. "What about you?"

"You're the food expert," he says folding the menu. "I'd rather have you order for me, if you don't mind."

"Sure. But only if you pick out the wine."

"You're on."

By the time the waiter places their entrees on the table, Dallas and Jillian are lost in conversation over the flickering candle between them. The waiter pours each a glass of wine and sets the bottle down.

"Lovely choice of wine, sir," the server says in earnest. Dallas nods proudly.

"This looks delicious," Jillian drools as the waiter disappears. Taking a bite, she savors its culinary delights. "And it is. So good. How do you like the baked Anelletti?"

"Never seen anything like this before. It's like a pasta cake." He digs into the mound of little pasta rings and discovers a gooey melted-cheese center. His face beams with his first taste. "Wow."

He offers her some on his fork which she happily nibbles.

"Heaven! I used to make this, but it's been years. I forgot how good it is."

"Have you ever thought of opening your own restaurant? You're just as good as this. If not better."

Jillian takes the flattery with a sip of wine but shrugs off the idea. "Thanks, Dallas. I used to think about it. A lot, actually. But it's too risky."

"How can you be so sure if you don't try? Give it a shot."

"Well, we looked into it a few years ago. Greg said the investment was too huge upfront. He didn't want to chance it."

"Because it was your dream not his," Dallas shakes his head, pissed at her ex-husband's selfishness. "Would you take the gamble now if you could?"

"Yes, but--"

"--No buts," he cuts her off. "No excuses. You want it, you go for it. Do you think baseball is a sure bet?"

"No, but you're so talented."

"So are you and in the end it doesn't matter, it's about determination and drive. It's a miracle I've made it this far, most guys don't. But I had to make the choice back when—risk everything to some day play in the majors or play it safe and sit behind a desk nine-to-five."

"You make it sound so easy."

"Didn't say it was easy, but it's better than living your life wondering 'what if'."

His support of her dream moves her more than she could ever put into words. No one, not her family nor her husband, ever rallied for her like this.

"What do you need to make it happen? Cash?"

"Yes, a good chunk of it," she folds her bare arms on the linen tablecloth and gets lost in his eyes. With Dallas's enthusiasm she believes she could do anything she put her mind to.

"Then get it. Anyone can get there hands on money," he declares almost challenging her while taking the napkin from his lap and placing it on the table. Her mind swims in the fantasy of her own restaurant as he finishes his wine—and to the investment maturing soon with Jonathan.

"Maybe it's time to think about it again. Thanks, Dallas." She moves her hand on top of his and gives it a little squeeze. Their new level of closeness courses through her veins. "Let's get out of here and get a drink across the street. Great jazz bar."

Dallas rolls his eyes.

"You don't like jazz I take it?"

"More of a classic rock guy, but," he stands up, walks over behind her and whispers in her ear, "Whatever you desire tonight, Miss Boston, it's your win."

# TWENTY-THREE

A tenor saxophone weeps while Jillian and Dallas wade through the busy dark nightclub and belly up to the bar.

"Decent size crowd for a weeknight," Dallas quips to the hip goateed bartender.

"These local guys have a big following. They've got a slight rock edge, brings in a whole different crew. What can I get for you?"

"Jack and Coke for me and," he defers to Jillian.

"Prosecco, thanks," she orders loudly against the song.

"Coming right up," the barkeep says as the bassist plucks the last note. The audience bursts into applause.

The stylish lead singer fits the microphone back in its stand and addresses his roomful of fans.

"Thanks for coming out tonight. We're going to take a short break. See you in a few."

The band rests their gear on stage; the trendy throng talks among themselves.

Dallas's eyes roam Jillian who tilts back her fluted glass of bubbly. Aware of his eyes all over her, she soaks in his attention. *This has been the perfect night, my dream date…he's so damn sexy in that suit…how am I ever going to let him leave?* She places the crystal stemware down on the bar and admires the streamlined décor of the club.

"Always loved this place."

"I'll admit it, it's pretty cool," he concedes then slides a gentle hand around her waist. The warmth of his hand on her bare low back is soothing—and intoxicating.

"Pretty famous for jazz and blues. A lot of greats played here."

"It's just that I don't dig that free form stuff, I like more of a steady beat, know what I mean? Sometimes jazz sounds like a radio stuck between two stations," he explains and she chuckles, "but these guys aren't too bad. That singer has a lot of Springsteen in him, actually."

"So you won't die on me if we stick around for the next set?"

Dallas shrugs then suddenly lurches forward as if pushed from behind; he turns around to find out who just stuck an elbow in his back.

"Here you go, Phil. You guys sound great tonight," the bartender slides a drink across the polished steel counter to the singer.

"Thanks, Charlie," Phil says, grabbing the bottle. He sees Dallas leering at him. "Sorry if I bumped you. Tight squeeze to get a drink tonight."

"It's cool. Hey, you know you kind of remind me of The Boss."

The singer's face lights up. "Love Bruce. Saw him in concert like a million times. He's the best. Period."

"Yeah, right? I saw him a couple times in DC. Nobody beats Bruce live."

"Nobody."

"So, no offense, but why this jazzy thing instead of rockin' out?"

"I got tired of the whole rock 'n roll circus. Just needed a change--new clubs, new faces. I guess you can't hide your influences no matter what you play."

Phil smiles at Jillian over Dallas's shoulder as she sits down on a stool. "Hey, I should let you get back to your girlfriend. Enjoy the show."

The suave crooner starts to walk away when Dallas stops him, "Hey, Phil, hold up a sec."

In his best man-to-man voice, Dallas asks, "Could you do me a favor? It's our first date. Well, sort of. Could you play something slow by Bruce so we can dance? Although he tries, Dallas's eyes can't hide he's got it bad for Jillian. "She'd like that."

"I'd love to help you out. But a Boss cover here? No can do, sorry," the singer apologizes genuinely.

Dallas downplays his request. "No worries."

Before Phil can respond, Dallas catches sight of a slick-haired man decked out in a silk suit about to make a move on Jillian; Dallas's chest puffs up and his face flashes red. "You're really into this girl," Phil calls it like he sees it.

Dallas's eyes are riveted on Mr. Suit who takes the barstool next to Jillian. He watches the guy start to chat her up. "Look, she's great and all, but it's just a casual thing, really," he tries to minimize his feelings for her but his actions speak louder than his words. "Thanks anyway, man." Dallas punches Phil with bromance appreciation before dashing off to intercept the competition.

Phil, a hopeless romantic, feels for Dallas. Scratching at his James Dean sideburns, he flips through a catalog of tunes in his head until he finds one.

"Wait up," he shouts then catches up to Dallas. "I've got an old song that might do the trick. My keyboardist knows it, that's if he isn't too drunk to remember it. Let me see what I can do for you, I mean for your girl." Phil winks.

Dallas reveals his true feelings when he says, "Thanks, Phil."

The two shake hands and the singer heads toward the stage.

Dallas abruptly cuts in and plants himself directly between Jillian and her wannabe-Wall Street suitor, giving his back to the guy. Although Jillian is relieved at being saved from Hedge Fund Henry, she is surprised and turned on, by Dallas's ballsy move. She hops up off the stool and motions toward the stage, "What was that all about?"

"Just shooting the shit about music. Nice guy," he spits out in monotone before becoming overly serious, barely containing hostility under his breath, "Why are you talking to this guy? You'd rather go home with him?"

She's shocked by the accusation--and his bizarre behavior. "Of course not, Dallas, why would you even—"

"Hey, buddy, I was talking to the lady first," Henry arrogantly interrupts.

Dallas, his body stiffening with rage, ignores him and locks his stare down on Jillian. She sees Henry's fuming face pop up from behind Dallas and shoot her a look that he's pissed at this young intruder. Predicting Henry's movement behind him, Dallas shifts his weight to his other leg to block Mr. Suit once again.

*This could get ugly real fast.*

Jillian places her palm on Dallas's chest for balance as she leans around the rigid trunk of her Minor Leaguer to politely let the guy down and save the peace, "Nice chatting with you, Henry, but I'm with him. Have a good night." The defeated man stomps off in a huff.

She returns to a chest-to-chest stance with Dallas. He backs away from her hand on him, leans over the bar, and orders a double shot. She lets him be. *He needs a little space right now to cool off...wow, never pegged him as the jealous type...looks like there's a whole lot of deep stuff churning through him right now. Someone must've hurt him badly.* He tosses back the whiskey, plunks the shot glass down hard on the bar, and stares forward off into who knows where in the past.

Jillian gently clasps his forearm, trying to refocus his attention back onto her. His doe-brown eyes silently tell her he's mad at himself for the outburst—and for letting his growing feelings toward her slip out. "Jilly, I'm—"

She doesn't let him finish. She flutters her eyelashes up at him to sweep away the negativity and recapture her romantic evening. "Why don't we get a table before the music starts?" she suggests sweetly. Dallas nods, takes her arm, and leads her across the noisy nightclub.

Just as they get seated, the musicians take the stage, pick up their instruments, and plug in to their amps. After a chat with the keyboard player, Phil takes his place at the front of the stage and adjusts his mike.

"We're back for our final set of the evening. Thanks, everybody, for sticking around. We're going to start off with a special request from a guy who wants to get up close to his girl here tonight. It's one of my songs from way way back called "Goodnight Romeo"."

The audience cheers while Phil cues the keyboardist who starts tinkling a dark and moody electric piano. The drummer taps a soft rat-a-tat-tat beat on the hi-hat. Several couples walk out onto the dance floor and embrace their way into a slow dance. A sultry guitar begins to wail a longing melody.

Dallas turns to Jillian with a charming smile. "Care to dance, gorgeous?"

"Love to," she responds.

He takes her by the hand and leads her to the center of the dance floor. He firmly clasps her right hand in his and pulls her to him. When she spies him give the singer a thumbs up over the back of her bare shoulder, she realizes Dallas had made the request.

Jillian presses her eyes shut and nestles her head next to his, listening to Phil's honey-filled voice. *This is all too perfect. Remember, Jillian, there is no tomorrow with Dallas, only now. Right now. Live in this moment.*

"...and I'm in the dark, just another stranger I'll never know, and I'm in her arms...," Phil sings.

Dallas and Jillian unify and rock to and fro as one, lost together in the music.

"...before the morning comes I'll go, slip past those honest eyes...,"

The bass line thumps as Dallas draws her near; her delicate hand sliding up behind his neck. The lyrics, their closeness, they both savor it all, afraid to give in to their true feelings.

"...I don't walk so tall in the darkness, but I'm not running for the light, and it's time to say goodnight to Romeo...,"

Jillian senses Dallas's heart opening as he leans down to press his cheek against hers; she fights herself to keep her heart from betraying the reality of tomorrow.

"...If you want me to say it, I'll be alright. If you need the truth, which truth would you like? It would've been nice not to have to say goodbye...," the singer's words hit home.

As the song winds down, Jillian's eyes mist, soaking in the feeling of his arms around her. She's in control of her heart, but barely; Dallas however is holding on to her for dear life, as if he'd never let her go.

"Wouldn't it be nice not to have to say goodbye?" Phil sings out again and again over the crescendo of the heavy-hearted ballad.

Back at home, Dallas leans against the hallway wall watching Jillian fumble for her keys. She feels him looking at her but their energy is different. *He feels it too, tonight we both let our guard down. I hoped for this more than I want to admit, and now that it's here...I can't...he'll be gone by next week...I can't make love with him tonight, too many emotions, I'll never be able to let go. I have to be the strong one.*

With her key chain finally in her grasp, she turns her gaze to him. His eyes are full of adoration as she says, "Dallas Monroe, you were the perfect date tonight. Thank you."

"It wasn't too tough with you on my arm."

She smiles, and says goodnight as she slides the key into the knob.

"Goodnight? You made that sound like the evening is over. We're just getting started, Miss Boston," Dallas get his sexy growl on and inches toward her.

But Jillian holds her ground. She walks through her door and gently, but strongly, prevents him from following her in with her hand. "Sorry, I don't sleep with a man on the first date. Policy. Nothing personal."

Dallas is out of his mind.

"Jilly, c'mon," he calls her bluff, urgency leaking out through his words, and doesn't budge. He gives her sincere eyes and the most honest voice he has, "I really want to be with you tonight."

She starts closing the door on him until he has no choice but to back up into the hall.

"I'll sleep over," he throws all his cards down on the table, his longing for her clearly consuming him.

She's astonished at his offer. But now, as much as she's desired sleeping in his arms all night and never wanted that--or him--more than she does right at this moment, she can't. For a second, she almost gives in. But she knows her heart would never withstand the heartache of losing him after that.

"Goodnight, Romeo," she says softly, shutting the door.

Inside, she leans her back against the door, listening to him on the other side of it, waiting, hoping she'll change her mind. It's excruciating.

After a long deafening-loud silence he says, "'Night, Jilly."

She listens to his defeated footsteps trudge down the hall.

*That was the hardest thing I've ever had to do.*

# TWENTY-FOUR

Russ removes the back of Josephine's computer tower. After some fiddling and diddling, he finds the problem.

"Looks like your motor burned out. No biggie. I'll have that fixed in a jiffy."

"So I won't get the day off with pay?"

"Afraid not," he says unscrewing parts of the hardware.

"Thanks for nothing, Russ," she needles him. "How's your wife doing? Feeling any better?"

"Not really. She's going in for surgery on Friday. Bad timing, I have tickets for Game Five. Box seats too. Know anyone who would like to buy them?"

Jillian, half-asleep at her desk from her big night out, perks up. "Did you say you have tickets? How many?"

"Didn't know you were a baseball fan," Russ chirps pleasantly surprised. "Four."

"Can I buy two?"

"Sure. I'll swing by later. They're good seats, but expensive."

"I don't care what they cost. This will be so great. Dallas can't possibly win if I do this."

Russ is confused. "But Dallas isn't playing in the Pennant Race."

Josephine clarifies, fluttering her jingly-blinged wrists followed by an exaggerated wink, "Dallas is a WHO, Russell, not a WHERE."

"What?" Russ asks, totally bewildered.

A floral delivery man knocks on the cubicle and enters with a large bouquet of exotic flowers in a ceramic vase.

"Look. At. Those," Josephine yells.

"Jillian Miles?" the florist asks, reading the card.

"That's me," she answers, jumping out of her high tech chair with joy.

After she signs for them, the delivery guy places the floral arrangement on her desk then leaves.

"Hurry up and open the card! As if we don't know who they're from," Josephine rushes her.

She reads it to herself first, then aloud, "You were astonishing last night. Dallas."

Jillian's glow is radiant and an infectious smile spreads ear-to-ear.

Josephine "Oh my God, I'm having a hot flash."

"It's any wonder you two get any work done around here," Russ laughs. "I'll be back with your motor and your tickets."

"I should text him and say thanks," Jillian says and grabs her phone without taking her eyes off the wild orange and purple flowers.

"Call him, don't text," Josie recommends, getting up to smell the lilies surrounding the tall-stemmed Birds of Paradise. "Make it a personal touch. He did." She inhales the glorious scent.

*She's right.* Jillian dials, not knowing his schedule, hoping he'll pick up.

"Hey there, gorgeous," he says, answering on the second ring. Her heart jumps at the sound of his voice.

"Dallas, thank you so much. They're beautiful."

"They pale in comparison to you. You know I thought about you all night...couldn't sleep a wink."

She can't look at Josephine who is acting like a love struck idiot over at her desk. "Stop it, " she silently mouths to her co-worker and turns away with a giggle.

She focuses her attention on Dallas's voice. "It was probably the espresso."

"It was probably your ass in that dress."

Jillian blushes but eats it up.

"I wanted you sooooo bad," his voice turns low and naughty. "Still do. Just thinking about it is making it throb. Meet me at my place in thirty?"

"I can't, I have an appointment this afternoon," Jillian says on the down-low so Josephine doesn't hear her, but she does anyway.

"You're killing me, Jilly. I have to see you. Come to my game tonight?"

"I'd love that."

"Cool. See you at six. Quincy Field."

"Okay. See you then."

She hangs up and does a one-eighty back toward her crazy colleague. "I'm gonna kill you one of these days, Josie," she warns. "Want to go to his game with me tonight?"

"If you're talking young studs in baseball pants, I'm so there."

Later that afternoon, when Jillian strides down Commonwealth Ave toward her lawyer's office, she passes a real estate company with multiple listings posted in the window. She stops to look for any possible sites for a restaurant. Her restaurant. Dallas reopened the door to her dream--and she, for the first time in control of her world, is gladly walking through it.

All she needs is the cash. And today she is going to get it.

"You realize, Jillian, you'll take a substantial penalty by opting for a cash payout."

"I know; my accountant went through everything with me on the phone this morning."

"You're being ridiculous," Greg snaps at her.

"Get over it," she puts her ex in his place. "Jonathan, when can I expect the distribution?"

"You should have the check in ten days or so after we dissolve the account."

"Perfect. I'm looking at a property, so sooner the better."

"I'll have the paperwork drawn up and couriered over to both of you ASAP. New house?"

"Commercial space."

"Well, good luck with your venture," he says genuinely as Greg scowls. "I think this wraps it up for today. If you'll excuse me, I'm due in court." He stands and gathers his papers into a leather portfolio.

"Thanks, Jonathan," Jillian says.

Greg shakes the lawyer's hand and asks, "Where's Finley Associates in this building? I have an appointment in fifteen minutes."

"Just down the hall. Ask my secretary if you can't find it. Good day," he bids them both and rushes out.

Once the attorney is out of ear shot, he lashes out at Jillian. "What is going on with you? Are you going through your change or something? Strip clubs and opening a restaurant? I don't even know you anymore."

His opinion---or anyone else's---of her really no longer matters. "The truth is, Greg, you never knew me. You never took the time to learn me," she counters, strutting out of the conference room door, flipping her hair over her shoulder all the while never looking back at him.

Greg hurriedly catches up to her in the hallway and follows her to the elevator. "Teach me then. Give me a second chance. I miss you. Your cooking, your way of making a house a home. And now suddenly you're so...so...damn sexy. I'll break it off with Kiki. Give us a second chance."

She ignores him completely. The door of the elevator opens, she saunters in and presses the button. Greg stands there in the lobby, watching her move with a powerful sensual grace that drives him wild. She looks at him with a triumphant stare as the elevator doors start to close, "Give Kiki my best."

# TWENTY-FIVE

On a quintessential Fall afternoon, Jillian and Josephine join baseball fans young and old who gather at an historic ball field that proudly maintains its original wooden benches and century-old scoreboard. *This is as Americana as you can get.* She inspects every uniformed player hoping he's her hot pitcher.

"There he is!" she elbows Josie while waving to Dallas to get his attention.

Josie, however, is totally distracted by the cute catcher who squats then rises up to throw the ball back to the pitcher. "Look at him. I could just nibble his bum," she exclaims before peeling her eyes off the young man to listen to Jillian. "Okay. Where's Loverboy?"

"Number twelve," Jillian points. Dallas finally sees her and waves.

"He's a cutie pie! No wonder you're all hot and bothered," she says truthfully. Josephine watches the body language exchange between Jillian and Dallas with an expert love guru's eye. When Dallas trots off to the mound she reels Jillian back down to Earth. "Okay, let's go grab a seat over by third base before they're all gone. You'll see him best from there."

The innings come and go and it's obvious to everyone watching this semi-pro game that Dallas Monroe is a star athlete.

"I've never seen him in his uniform. So sexy."

"Not only that, he actually lives up to it. He's a top-notch player."

"It's his true passion. I love watching in his element."

Strike out after strike out, thanks to Dallas, his team is way ahead of their visiting opponent.

By the top of the ninth, many people start filing out of the bleachers to beat the parking lot rush after the game.

"Do you mind staying, Jo? I want to talk to him before we leave."

"No problemo. Let's head over to the fence near the dug out."

After carefully scooting down the bleachers, the women make their way around the field when someone calls her name. "Jillian? Is that you?"

Among the crowd of fans exiting the park, she sees her cousin and flags him over. "Peter!"

He breaks free from the stream of spectators and walks over to them. He gives her a big hug which she readily accepts. "Oh my God I haven't seen you in ages," the attractive man says gleefully. "Sorry I missed the fundraiser. Work has been nuts."

"Same old, same old. You didn't miss a thing, believe me."

"Since when are you a baseball fan?"

Before she can answer him, Josie tugs on her jacket and gives her a heads up, "Loverboy is looking for you."

Dallas stands close to the chain link fence, staring at her and Peter without a smile.

"Pete, hold on a sec. I have to talk to someone. Don't leave," she makes him promise.

Thrilled, she bolts over to Dallas who, with suspect eyes, looks put off.

"You were great!" she enthusiastically compliments him but he and his tight-jawed expression ignore it.

"Who's he?" he nods his head toward Peter, seemingly gritting his teeth.

"Peter?" she asks, detecting jealousy in his tone. She placates his worry with a lighthearted voice, "He's my cousin, Dallas. Growing up we were always best friends. We haven't seen each other in a long time."

He studies her response to make sure she's telling the truth, making her feel as though she's being interrogated under a CIA spotlight. A teammate walks behind him and pats him on the back. "Nice game, bro." The interruption breaks him free from his train of thought and lets his jealousy go. His face relaxes, showing her he believes her and that he's glad she came.

"Guess what?" she exclaims. "I got us tickets to Game Five tonight!"

"Are you serious?"

"They're box seats. That's good, right?"

"Good? Even Uncle Jack can't get those in a Pennant Race game. Holy shit."

"Alright, meet me at my place in an hour?"

"I'm there."

"This is going to be fun," she waves goodbye with her eyes lit up and hurries back over to Peter and Josephine.

"I'd love to stay and chat, Jillian, but I really gotta run. Can we do dinner next week and catch up?"

"I'd love that. I don't think I have your number."

Peter fishes a business card out of his wallet and hands it to her.

"You're doing commercial real estate now?" she asks, thrilled at the timing. "We so have to talk. I'll call you tomorrow." She gives him another hug and kiss on the cheek.

"It was nice meeting you, Josephine."

"Likewise," she replies before he jogs off toward the exit. Jillian and Josephine follow the same route but at a leisurely pace.

"What was that all about with Loverboy?" Josephine probes, not wasting any time.

"You don't miss a thing, do you?" Jillian scoffs. "He wanted to know who Peter was."

"If you painted that boy bright green from head-to-toe he couldn't have looked more jealous."

"I saw that side of him come out at the bar last night."

"Well, the way he looked at you with Peter, and the flowers today, there is no doubt in my mind that Loverboy has way more feelings for you than he's admitting. To you or to himself."

"I want to believe that's true. And I want to be with him more than anything, but Josie, what are we going to do? He leaves really soon."

"Frequent-flyer miles are the aphrodisiac of the twenty-first century."

"I've thought about that, and wouldn't mind traveling, but he'll never be in the same city for more than a night," she sighs with a tormented heart. "I just don't know how this is going to work out," she sadly mumbles, kicking a small rock as they leave the baseball field.

# TWENTY-SIX

Copley Stadium is a madhouse full of Boston's most-faithful, rowdiest baseball fans. For the Cougars tonight it's either win and stay alive or lose the championship here at home; the adrenalin is palpable.

Plowing through rows of plastic stadium seats, Jillian's wool poncho gets caught on an arm rest and almost knocks her off balance. Dallas, close behind, is quick to help her out. "Whoa, hold on there, Superhero, you can't fly and fight crime if your cape is stuck," he cautions, releasing the blue paisley fabric from its trap. They continue on to find their premium seats.

"Excuse us," Jillian says to the family of six they nearly crawl over to get to their designated chairs. Seated at last, Dallas can't get over their view. "We can see in the dugout from here! Unbelievable."

"Not bad for my first Cougars game, huh?"

"Jilly, whenever you do something first, you really do it."

"It seems that way," she takes the compliment with a proud grin.

A vendor selling refreshments makes his way up the aisle toward the pair who are getting comfortable in their narrow seats.

"Two super-size drinks and," he looks to Jillian for her food choice.

"That's all for me, thanks."

"What?! No. You can't come to a baseball game, a final championship game, and not have a hot dog. That's a crime. It's un-American."

"Okay, okay," she laughs.

The vendor hands them their goodies. But before Dallas places his 24 oz cup down, she offers him a toast with her own. "Here's to the next time I'm watching a game here...when you'll be out there pitching."

"I'll drink to that," he says all-smiles as they clunk plastic cups.

They sit looking around, taking in the ball park which appears at almost crowd capacity at this point.

"So, what are the chances that St. Louis makes a come back tonight and wins this?" she asks.

"Listen to you sounding like a baseball professional," he rides her, placing his hand on her knee and leaning his body toward her. She wraps her hand around his and angles herself left towards him, as close to him as she can. "This is anybody's game tonight," Dallas speculates.

But by the top of the eighth inning, it turns out to be Boston's game. Ahead by a landslide, the Cougars have this one in the bag; their shot at the title still possible.

"Boston played great ball tonight," Dallas comments, impressed. "So glad I got to see it."

"So glad I got to win it," she points out saucily.

"At this point, looks like you did. Can't wait to get home," he grins with delight.

"Why wait?" She smirks and leans all the way over to him to whisper in his ear, "I'm not wearing any underwear. Feel for yourself."

Before he can react, from under her poncho she guides his hand up to her unzipped jeans to prove it.

He's totally turned on, but freaking out. "Are you crazy? There are a million security cameras in here, they'll zoom right in on us. We'll get arrested."

"They won't see anything if we do it right," she playfully coerces him and pushes his hand into her pants.

"Or worse, we'll go viral on the Internet. Oh my God, there goes my career."

She laughs but insists, "My win."

"Your win," he repeats, unable to deny that the incognito of this tryst only adds gasoline to his burning desire. He can't resist petting the smooth skin above her pubes, away from the unknowing eyes around them.

"Don't know why you're complaining, you have the easy part. I have to keep my calm like nothing's happening."

"Oh yeah, real easy. At least your covered. Like I'm going to be able to hide a big hard-on."

The both nervously chuckle. Until she directs his fingers inside her moist mound.

"Oh fuck," he groans, scanning the people sitting around them to see if anyone can tell he's thumbing her clit.

Her hips buck from his clandestine circular strokes on her sweet spot. *Dammit that feels good. Almost too good.* "Don't stop," she orders him through short shallow breaths. She grabs her drink and sucks on the straw to disguise her ever-building excitement.

A few rows down in front of them, a chubby man in a Boston Cougars hoodie rises to his feet, as do the members of his family, to get out of Dodge like many of the fans, satisfied that the Cougars will win.

"Oh no, that's Mike. He works for Uncle Jack. Please don't see me. Please," Dallas prays while she is on fire next to him, hardly able to contain herself from the impending massive orgasm that is within moments of overtaking her.

So he's not recognized, Dallas turns his head when the big man is about to pass by. He looks at Jillian who is barely holding herself together and practically chewing her soda straw. Dallas's dilemma makes this only hotter for her, if that's even physically possible.

"Dallas, is that you?" Mike calls out.

"Oh shit," Dallas closes his eyes for a split second in both fear and erotic bliss.

Under the poncho Jillian aggressively holds his hand in place to finish his illicit task. "If you stop now I swear I'll never have sex with you again."

Dallas bites his bottom lip and pivots to Mike, deepening his fingers inside this once Virgin Mary next to him. "Hey, Mike, how's it going?"

"Great, thanks. Good win for Boston, huh? Hey, you know that short stop we tried out from Philly yesterday? You think he's gonna make the cut? I kinda have my doubts."

Dallas crosses his legs in an attempt to hide the unstoppable erection which is growing by the second as she wriggles from the swirling of his middle finger as far down into her love box he can reach.

"I like the guy from Michigan better. I guess we'll see in the scrimmage tomorrow," Dallas blurts out barely able to concentrate on what he's saying. Perspiration beads now pop out across his forehead.

Mike gives him a funny look. "Guess so. Hey, are you feeling okay? You look a little, I don't know," he inquires unable to put his finger on it.

But Dallas is all fingers on it and about to pull out of Jillian's sex when she digs her nails into the back of his hand to force him to finish her off.

"Just overtired. Long week," Dallas tries to convince him while Jillian deep throats the plastic straw as she surrenders to the mind-blowing climax happening between her thighs.

"Yeah, I here ya. Get some sleep, buddy. I'll see you tomorrow." Mike says, taking off to catch up to his family.

Dallas, relieved that is over, slumps in the high-priced seats as he withdraws his hand from her spasming pussy. He turns back to a sweaty Jillian who zips up her jeans with no one near them the wiser.

"Oh my God," he exclaims.

"You're not kidding. I don't think I can walk right now," she giggles with euphoria bursting through her body.

"I know I can't," Dallas complains but loves it, calling her attention to his bulging crotch. "This is fucking agony right here. Good thing we have another inning."

"I'll make it up to you, I promise."

"Yeah, well, payback is a bitch if, no when, I win the next game. Come over here, You." He gives her lovey dovey bedroom eyes. She leans in and kisses her lovingly on the lips then her forehead. They both feel it, but neither of them can say it aloud.

Exhausted from their big night at Copley Stadium, they sit in bumper-to-bumper traffic after the game. Neither one minds or is in any hurry; they are quiet and peaceful, content being together holding hands and listening to the radio.

Eventually they make it back to their apartment complex. Dallas pulls in a spot, parks, and shuts off the engine. *Huh, he usually drives me right to the door, but that's okay.* She waits for her goodnight kiss, knowing better at this point to hope for anything more.

"What time is your flight tomorrow?" she asks.

"Eight something."

"I can drive you if you want. I don't mind."

"That's a pretty damn early start, are you sure? "

"I'm sure. I can get Baxter at the same time."

"You are the best."

"So I've heard."

"I knew it would all go to your head one of these days," he smirks sweetly before kissing her.

But this is a different kiss. Void of carnal lust and primal intentions, it's tender and affectionate. It's an exchange of emotions between a couple who can't be a couple, but who want to be one more than either can articulate. Despite their imminent separation, they give in to their feelings for each other before their lips part.

"How about I get Baxter and stay over tonight? It'll save us time in the morning."

More than just a little pleasantly surprised, she looks into his beautiful vulnerable eyes. *I'm done protecting my future heart. I'm living for now. All we have is this moment..and I want it all. No regrets.*

"Don't forget your toothbrush," she answers cheekily.

In the middle of the night, they lie entwined. Jillian rests curled up inside his big muscular arms that wrap tightly around her. Her chin nuzzles perfectly in his neck. Neither sleep soundly, preferring to stay half-awake to bask in the rarity of being together.

"We'll figure us out, Jilly. I promise," he mumbles in his pillow voice. Kissing the top of her head, he pulls her close to his chest.

She returns his kiss on the nape of his neck. Jillian then rolls him onto his back and crawls on top of him. Looking down into his eyes, she loves his soft touch when he brushes her hair out of her face and runs the back of his hand down her profile.

"Long distance isn't that hard anymore, right? Phones, computers, cheap flights," she argues.

"We'll manage. The road is tough on baseball families, though. I see how the other guys struggle. It's hard to keep up with a moving target. Are you sure you're up for that?"

"Just watch me," she swears to him and leans down to passionately kiss him to seal the deal.

She then rests her head on his chest, swaddled in his big arms, and closes her eyes. He tenderly caresses her back in a slow rhythm. It's so soothing and hypnotic that after a few minutes she can't help but completely unwind and fall fast asleep.

# TWENTY-SEVEN

"Sorry, Peter. Have you been waiting long?" Jillian hugs her dear cousin who stands on a pristine main street in affluent Chestnut Hill, a swanky village just a few miles west of Boston.

"No, just got here myself. No worries. Are you ready?"

"I can't wait."

Peter unlocks a vacant restaurant door which bears the sign "Now Leasing". Jillian waltzes inside, hopeful this is where the next chapter of her life will unfold. Following her in, he stands aside to let his cousin take in the space. First impressions are everything.

Immediately the charm of the place grabs her. *Look at that.* She gravitates to the antique wooden bar, its fine craftsmanship well-preserved and too irresistible not to touch. Fine mahogany carvings and turnings, it's truly an aesthetic treasure. *It's not hard to imagine the barkeeps tending here a hundred years ago.*

"The property comes with a beer and wine license. If you want to add hard liquor, we can apply for that. Costly, but not impossible to obtain."

"It's exquisite, Peter. I love it," she says, walking behind its varnished bar counter. From that vantage point she takes in the whole dining area; her mind races with décor and menu ideas.

"Seats about fifty guests inside and about a twenty, comfortably, on the back terrace. Want to see the kitchen?"

"Yes," she answers eagerly and follows him toward the back of the Boston landmark property.

"The last tenant had all the commercial grade refrigeration updated just last year." He walks her around, pointing everything out. "Rotisserie oven, convection oven, char-broiler. And you'll love this," he opens a back door to small hall. "Walk-in freezer AND walk-in cooler."

"It has everything I want and it's the perfect size. Can I see the patio?"

The cousins step out onto a terracotta brick terrace surrounded by painted trellises and covered overhead with wooden lattice flush with withered vines and wisteria from seasons past. *Add some little white lights and live acoustic music, this would be magical on a summer's night.*

Peter pulls out a wrought iron cafe chair and sits at a small cafe table. "Take your time. I'm just going to check my messages," he says and takes out his phone.

Jillian continues to stroll around, inspecting every nook and cranny. *I could put a small bar over there. Potted French lavender, maybe, as accents. I could do a small plates or tapas menu...oh, I love it. I want this place.*

"So what do you think? I have another listing in Cambridge that's in the same price range if you want to take a look at that."

"No. This feels like home," she says with absolute certainty as she sits down at the table across from him. "Let's do this."

Still on a high from signing the purchase and sales agreement a few hours earlier, Jillian sits at her dining room table at home, flipping through cookbooks and interior design magazines for inspiration for her new endeavor. *I can't believe I'm actually doing it.* She turns down the corner of a page on couscous jumbalaya. *If Dallas hadn't come into my life, I wouldn't have done this. I would never have had the courage or gumption...I owe him a lot.* She takes a sip of vintage Napa Valley wine, one she knows is Dallas's personal favorite and remembers how much sweeter it tasted on his lips. *He'll be proud of me...I'm proud of me...but I'll wait until it's all official before I tell him. It'll be a fun surprise, I'll bring him to...to...what am I going to call it?...well, to the restaurant and have a champagne toast...hopefully it'll happen before he's gone out West.*

Feeling on top of the world, she refuses to let the thought of him living far away from her get her down. *Don't go there, Jillian. That's in the future. He'll be here tonight, right here. That's all that really matters right now.* She looks at the time. *Game Six starts in two hours. I better marinate the meat for dinner tonight.* She closes up her books and slips them back in their places on her bookshelf before heading into the kitchen.

# TWENTY-EIGHT

With Dallas watching the game in the other room, Jillian is in her glory preparing her favorite seasonal dinner.

"I'm starving," Dallas says as he saunters into the kitchen during a time out. Spinning his baseball cap backwards, he sticks his nose in the saucepan. "God that smells incredible."

"Won't be long," Jillian promises then nudges him out of the way to grate a tiny dark ball over the simmering soup. Dallas can't make out what she's doing. "Fresh nutmeg. Secret to my butternut squash bisque." She takes a deep whiff of the freshly ground spice. "Mmmm. Almost sexual."

"Anything with you is sexual as far as I'm concerned."

"Hand me that potholder?" she asks, opening the oven door. A wave of roasted lamb escapes as he hands it to her.

"Oh man. You're going to send me care packages if I go to Arizona, right?"

"No way," she firmly asserts holding back a smile while basting the fingerling potatoes with the meaty au jus. After closing the range door, she turns the dial to broil.

"No? And here I thought you liked me."

"How else am I going to entice you back here to visit?"

Dallas gives her a loving squeeze on her derriere. "I can think of something."

"Not so fast." She gives him a step back stare. "Has St. Louis won?" She strains to see the TV. "Nope. Seventh inning. Boston. Hands off."

Dallas lets go, enjoying her sass. "Brutal."

A cell phone rings.

"That's mine," Jillian says wiping her hands on her apron and picking it up off the counter. "Oh, I should take this," she says suggesting she needs privacy.

"Alright, the game's back on. Holler if you need me," he slaps her on the ass. "And even if you don't."

When he's out of ear shot, Jillian takes the call with a hushed voice. "Hi, have you heard anything from Jonathan?"

Greg sounds miffed. "Hi Jillian. Yes, I got the paperwork today. But this is just a bad move on your part. I talked to Roger my financial advisor and he's got some safe annuities--"

She cuts him off without apology. "It's not unsafe and it's my decision. Send me the documents, Greg."

"I'm only trying to save you from yourself."

"I don't need your saving. My life is my own now and you have no business telling me how to run it."

She realizes her voice is getting too loud and looks in on Dallas who is glued to the TV.

"I need...I want my papers by tomorrow."

"If you'd just listen to reason."

She sees Dallas hop up during another time out and heading toward her and the kitchen.

"Tomorrow." She hangs up and shuts off her phone.

He senses her agitation. "What was that all about?"

She doesn't want to lie. "It was Greg, my ex-husband."

Dallas's face flares with a contained but simmering jealousy. "Why are you talking to him?"

"We have an old financial matter that came up. He's fighting me on it."

"I'm not sure I like you talking to him."

"Dallas, be serious," she makes light of it.

"I am."

"He is the last person I am interested in talking to. Trust me," she asserts firmly, giving him a look that makes him back down.

"Okay, okay, I trust you," he shrugs it off. "Dinner ready?"

"Just about."

Jillian shuts off the broiler, takes the roasting pan out of the oven, and pushes it to the back of the cook top to cool. Reaching for soup bowls in the cupboard, Mimi and Baxter scamper into the kitchen and whine to go out.

"Let me take these two gremlins out and I'll go grab a Beaujolais from my place. Been saving it for a special occasion, would pair perfectly with this."

*Little does he know what a special day this has been.* "Perfect." He kisses her on the cheek then steals a warm, freshly-baked buttermilk biscuit and wolfs it down before she can stop him.

"Hey!"

"Deeeee-lish. Okay, c'mon you guys."

The three race to the door where the dogs wag their tails waiting to get leashed. *If I could live in this moment forever I would.*

Dallas scrapes up every last morsel on his plate before putting it down on the coffee table. The dogs beg with hopeful eyes. "Sorry, kids, too good to miss a drop."

"I'll give them something after the game—which looks soon by the way Boston is playing tonight."

"Yeah, yeah, yeah," Dallas leans back on the couch and puts his arm around Jillian who snuggles next to him. Looking over at the picture window across the room, he finds it odd she's taken down all the drapes and left it bare except for the blinds. "What's up with the curtains?"

"It's time to get the winter drapes up. Had a heck of time getting the wooden rod back up, though. I'll work on it tomorrow."

"Guys are good for that stuff, ya know. You should've called me. I'm always happy to help you out."

The TV announcer and Cougars fans go wild. Boston wins Game Six.

Dallas picks up his wine glass and says, "Victory is yours again, gorgeous. But please, I beg you, I made it through jazz, pleeeeease no opera."

She chuckles. "Madame Butterfly can wait, you're safe."

"Thank you," he exhales through his words.

"Well, at least from her," Jillian flirts.

"Oh?" Dallas's eyebrow arches. "Liking the sound of that," he growls low and gravelly with desire, "I can make you sing like that, baby." He runs his hand down her belly into her lap. She stops his fingers with a no-nonsense grip and stares him dead in the eye.

"We know you can. But, it's my win…and I think it's time to find out just how much I can make you sing. I want you on the bed. Naked. Pronto!"

"Damn I love being a sex slave for a hot woman."

"You are my sex slave," she orders.

"No need to tell me twice," he hops up off the couch and sprints into the next room like lightning. That sumptuous sound of Dallas unzipping his jeans followed by him bouncing on her mattress ramps up her momentum—and longing.

"Alright, you two sit still," she says to Mimi and Baxter before she gets up and crosses the room. From underneath her desk she pulls out a large glossy Libida Lux shopping bag. The dogs scrutinize her every move.

She's about to undress when it dawns on her that she's on display for all her neighbors to see. *Oops, better draw the blinds.* Walking over to do just that, she accidentally knocks over the twelve-foot long curtain rod leaning against the sill. While picking up the weighty wooden pole, a crazy thought occurs to her. She smiles wickedly. *Should I?* She bites her lip with an image blazing in her dirty mind.

"Hey, did you fall asleep in there?" he taunts her from the bedroom.

She doesn't respond. She drops the blinds and then her jeans.

"Jillian, don't make me come out there and get you."

"You stay on that bed and wait," she barks in voice that makes the dogs sit up frozen at attention.

"Yes, ma'am," he complies.

Jillian fully undresses and removes the contents of the bag: the leather bodysuit that once frightened her now fits her sexuality like a glove. From the coat closet she takes out a pair of red thigh high patent leather boots with heels so high and sharp they could strike oil in the fields of Texas. She slides the outfit on and zips up its front as if it was made for her. The fire engine red boots, a total guilty pleasure purchase, glide on easily and up to the middle of her quads. Her in-charge attitude is almost complete, except for one more thing.

She struts over to the window and grabs the freestanding cherry wood drapery dowel with one hand and smacks in down hard in the palm of her other hand. Mimi and Baxter race off into the kitchen to hide.

On her way to the bedroom, she stops and studies herself in the mirror from head to pointy patent leather toe. Emanating from a place deep in her soul, a brazen self-assured smirk wells up and blossoms across her face. *Who knew?*

She strides confidently into the bedroom with the rod in hand, then stops dramatically at the foot of the bed. Dallas, who's been lying about lackadaisically waiting for her, bolts up in bed at the sight of her.

"Jillian?!" he asks, dumbfounded and speechless with eyes straining to believe what they are seeing. "Holy fuck!"

"Get on your feet," she instructs him, tapping the wooden pole repeatedly on her palm.

Dallas, his mind blown, sits gawking at this domineering sensual creature and is slow to react.

"Don't make me tell you again," she warns him in a sharper voice. "Get up."

"Yes, ma'am." He does as he's told and marches his butt-naked self over to the foot of the bed where she waits for him, pointing to where she wants him to stand.

"What are you going to do with that?" he inquires flippantly, nodding at the rod.

"Shut up. From now on you speak only when I tell you to. Now turn."

He hesitates a moment too long.

"I told you to TURN."

"I love a hot bossy bitch," he manages to throw in before he follows her order.

"You'll pay for your insolence. Quiet!"

Ogling his tremendously sculpted backside, however, momentarily sidetracks her; she loses her train of thought in his flawless masculine form.

"Are you still back there?" the smart ass cracks, bringing her back to the task at hand.

She slaps him on his bare butt with the end of the pole.

"Quiet! Arms raised out to your sides, shoulder height. Do it."

He lifts his rippling biceps and triceps in the air after which she presses the wooden dowel horizontally into the small of his back and holds it there parallel to the floor.

"Arms down behind then under the bar, until palms face front. Do it." He wraps his limbs around the pole until it rests in the crook of each elbow. "Now face me."

He, her very own personal Vitruvian Man come to life, spins around wondering what the hell she's up to.

She steps up to him, her face inches from his chest, and tongue-kisses the lovely divot at the base of his neck. Her trail of kisses ultimately end up at his nipple where she licks the pink flat circle of flesh around it. Dallas's breathing grows erratic like it does when a man notches up from turned on to aroused. It's then he realizes what she's done—restrained by the long pole, he's defenseless and unable to use his arms.

While roaming his ripped abs with her hands, she sucks on his nipple which hardens and pops up full round. She flicks her tongue on the top of the sensitive little pea and torments it even more with her teeth. Dallas, growing harder by the second, is having a very difficult time standing there keeping still. Without intending to, he steps backwards--and away from her suckling mouth.

"Oh, that won't do at all. You're mine. All mine," she reminds him before placing both her palms on his chest and with all her might heaves him and his wooden rod backward onto the bed.

After landing with a bounce, he tries to raise him arms. He can't. "Shit! I can't fucking move at all," he surrenders with a smile, happy to be the recipient of her desires.

"Shut up and count your blessings you're lying face up."

He lovingly gives her a warning, "You just wait til the tables are turned, baby."

She takes a long look at her captive nude lover, her erotic playground, which, up until now she hasn't truly had the time to explore. Her naughty adventure starts by crawling over him, just enough above him to feel the heat of his body warm her chest and stomach. She teases him with an occasional tickling of her hair tips on his soft skin or brushing her breasts up against him as she devours his mouth for an out-of-this world French kiss.

She leaves his lips wanting and wriggles her way back down his extraordinary body, fingering every intricate line of his overly-defined trunk, one muscle group at a time. Dallas's body twitches from her touch and his breathing becomes thready. She loves his beautiful body. Without any rhyme or reason, she kisses this spot, licks that one, in a seemingly never-ending anatomical expedition. *He's a virtual roadmap of lust...and this leg of the tour is scheduled only one way: south.*

At the foot of the bed, her patent leather boots crinkle loudly as she kneels before his jewels. Dallas knows he's about to go for the carnal ride of his life. Fascinated by his male sex, she fondles his scrotum delicately like it's a cherished fragile Christmas ornament. Upon her firm clasp of it, his hanging fruit stiffens. Dallas's begging pleases her and challenges her to explore more of this private wonderland to see what exactly it is that excites him.

Her tongue then discovers a seam on the softest part of his ball sack which, measuring by the loud moans coming from its owner, is an incredibly sensitive sexy area. She torments him there over and over, until her lips find the next sweet zone right under the base of his now extremely hard shaft.

The pain and pleasure of where she's got him is almost too much for him to bear. His body writhing, Dallas pleads for mercy as he tries unsuccessfully to free his hands.

"Jillian, baby, please. I can't take this much longer."

She continues to tease and lick, pull and rub his privates causing Dallas to let out primal howls from an erotic state he's never visited until now.

Feeling her mission is accomplished below his Mason-Dixon line, Jillian wants him in the worst way. All of him. But before she lets him loose, Dallas, now a crazed and throbbing lunatic, breaks free on his own after doing an ab crunch that only a serious athlete can do. He throws the wooden pole across the bedroom like a javelin. His wild eyes stare her down like a wolf in heat. "Now who's in charge?"

*Oh shit.*

Despite her meek attempts to elude capture, he picks her up and throws her down on the bed, pinning her to it with his muscular frame. She loves feeling his full weight on her. He kisses her mouth hard, grinding his pelvis against hers, teasing her, knowing she wants him inside her. But suddenly he stops, which is pure agony for both of them.

"I want to feel your skin. Get this thing off," he pants, taking off the boots fast then trying to unzip the bodysuit. He's too frenzied to maneuver it so just takes it in his bare hands and starts ripping it and tearing it off her until she's naked. His sweaty body slides on top of her wanting flesh. She wraps her legs around his waist and he stares down at her with a face she's never seen. When he plunges himself into her, they both scream and moan at the impact—screams neither of them stop until the ferocious libidinous ride comes to its vigorous climax.

Exhausted and exhilarated after they reach their final destination, Dallas rolls off of her and onto a pillow to regain his breath. They're both wrecked. When the lovers' heart rates finally come down below stroke level, he reaches his hand over and rests it affectionately on her quivering belly.

"Oh my God. Who are you? And what have you done with Jillian Miles?" He teases her but deliriously impressed with this brand-new side of her.

She laughs and rolls over into his side. "I think you just met the real Jillian Miles for the first time. I know I did."

# TWENTY-NINE

In the middle of the afternoon, Jillian is happily lost in her own world, perfecting a balsamic reduction for lamb chops in her kitchen. An untried recipe, it's coming out pretty well so far.

An unexpected knock on her door startles her. "Just a minute," she yells, attempting to keep her culinary creation from burning.

Whoever it is knocks again impatiently.

"Okay, okay. Coming," she gives in and turns the heat off. *I'll try it again later.*

She takes off her apron and goes to find out who is interrupting her sacred research time. Peering through the peephole, she can't believe who she sees. She opens the door, annoyed as hell.

"Greg, what are you doing here?"

Her ex-husband walks in before he's invited, as if he's on a rescue mission. He hands Jillian a large Manilla envelope. Despite the fact he's here to give her the paperwork she's been waiting for, his presence in her place feels toxic.

"I signed all the papers. I won't hold you up any more."

Jillian takes the win with silent grace. The thought of her new restaurant soon becoming a reality makes her smile triumphantly deep inside.

"Thank you. I'll get them back to Jonathan tomorrow," she states and tries ever-so-politely to nudge him out the door.

Greg, however, has no intention of leaving. He wanders farther into her apartment and looks around at everything. He's edgy with an undercurrent of anger that makes her feel unsafe. He picks up a ceramic vase off a shelf. "I remember when you bought this in Cancun. I hated it," he says drowning in memories and puts in back down. "Still do."

Mimi charges out of the bedroom and sniffs him. Her little ears perk up like he's an intruder. He is, in a way. Greg inspects the bar and picks out a bottle of red wine, one of Dallas's. "This is good stuff. Do you mind?" He asks, uncorking the Beaujolais Nouveau before she gives him the green light.

Jillian, frozen like a deer in the headlights, is unsure of what to do or say to get him to leave—or why he's sticking around. Mimi picks up on the growing tension and starts whining.

Greg practically guzzles the glass of vintage wine. "I've left Kiki," he divulges.

Jillian picks up Mimi to quiet her.

Greg refills the glass to the brim and walks over to face Jillian. "I told her all I want is to have you back. And that's the truth."

She shouldn't for all he's put her through, but she feels sorry for him. Jillian is kind but firm when she spells it out for him, "I'm sorry, Greg, no. I've moved on. So should you."

Greg grows loud and upset. "You call this moving on? This whole place could fit in our old garage," he shouts, waving his arm across the living room--which Mimi perceives as a threat to her mom. The protective little Westie leaps out of Jillian's arm in a full-on attack.

"Mimi!" Jillian yells, unable to hold her as she flies and pounces on Greg.

Red wine sloshes out of his glass and splatters all down the front of her ex's white starched shirt. "Fucking dog!" he screams, pulling at the wet shirt while Mimi continues to bark at him.

"Mimi! Stop! I'm sorry, I'll get you a damp towel," she says.

"That' not going to do any good," he grumbles totally pissed off while he unbuttons his wine-stained shirt. "Where's your bathroom?"

"Off the bedroom, in there." She points.

Greg takes off his shirt as he crosses the living room.

Just as Greg disappears from sight, there's a rap on the door. *Now what?*

Dallas bursts in. "I got it! I made the team in Phoenix! Fall Ball, baby!" he tells her with more jubilance than she's ever seen on his sweet young face.

"Dallas," she tries to warn him about Greg but his adrenalin rush cuts her off.

He embraces her. "You'll come out to see me, right?"

He's just about to kiss her when Greg, naked from the waist up, walks out of the bedroom.

"Who the hell are you?" Greg demands to the muscular young athlete whose face goes white in disbelief at the sight of a half-dressed man coming out of his lover's bedroom.

"Who the fuck are you?" Dallas loses his shit.

"I'm Jillian' ex-husband," Greg boasts competitively.

Jillian watches her beloved Dallas fall from Cloud Nine and land on cement like a crystal vase. Even if he could conceal that kind of rage, that level of betrayal, Dallas isn't at all interested in trying.

"Sorry I interrupted," he throws his hands up, hurt and anger overwhelming him.

"Dallas, it's not what you think," Jillian insists with panic in her voice.

He looks at her riddled with pain, "I never thought you'd do this to me, not you, Jillian. You're just like her. I'm so out of here." He storms out, enraged and crushed to smithereens.

"Dallas, wait!" she yells after him, desperate to explain.

But the devastated star athlete puts as much distance between them as he can...and fast. She follows him out to the parking lot, still calling out to him. Furious and betrayed, he peels out in his Cherokee, leaving her standing heartbroken in the dusty air.

# THIRTY

Josephine and Jillian sit in the bleachers, watching Dallas's game. He's playing recklessly and taking his bad mood out on everyone on the field.

"He's going to hurt somebody if he doesn't calm down," Josie says, concerned.

"I just need to talk to him, but he won't listen to me. He won't take my calls or answer his door. He leaves in two days. I can't let it end like this. I can't let it end, period."

It's Dallas's turn up at bat. The pitcher throws him a fastball and he swings wildly and misses, his bat coming dangerously close to hitting the catcher squatting behind him. The catcher says something that Dallas doesn't like and a fight breaks out. The umpire calls time out and trots over to break apart the two players who are up in each other's faces. Dallas gets benched to cool off.

"This has to stop. Watch my bag?" She pushes her purse next to Josephine before climbing down the bleachers. Making her way through the spectators, she calls out through the chain link fence to Dallas who paces angrily in the dugout.

He sees her and his mood turns even darker. He won't acknowledge her existence.

"Dallas, please, let me explain! Please!" she pleads, not caring that everyone in the dugout hears her.

His teammates gawk at her then him, but Dallas won't give her the satisfaction of looking in her direction. When the coach puts him back in, he gladly runs off into the field and away from her.

Funneling all his anger from the mound, his pitches fly fast and hard. He nearly pegs a batter with a curve ball. Dallas has lost all control of his emotions.

In the bottom of the next inning, he's up at bat and hits a line drive up the middle. He runs to first when the center fielder misses the catch. Taking his chances, Dallas tries for second and makes it. He looks to center field to see the player has just retrieved the ball. He goes for third. The pitch comes in and he knows it's going to be close—he hurls himself forward and slides toward third when the baseman leaps into the air to catch the ball. With no place to go other than on top of base stealing Dallas Monroe, the stocky third baseman lands full-weight on Dallas's outstretched pitching arm.

Dallas screams in agony.

"Daaaaalllllaaaaaas!!!" Jillian shrieks, her fingers rattling the chain link fence which prevent her from running to him.

The coach and umpire sprint over to Dallas who rolls on the ground, yelling in pain. The officials wave over the paramedics as his teammates empty the dug out and surround their hurt buddy. The concerned spectators stand on their feet, watching quietly as the EMTs carry Dallas Monroe off the field on a stretcher to a waiting ambulance.

Jillian, sobbing hysterically, pushes her way through the exiting fans to find Josephine. Her friend and co-worker is one step ahead of her, waiting at a side exit with her purse. "Let's go. They'll take him to Charlton Hospital. I'll drive."

# THIRTY-ONE

"Are you family?" the stern nurse behind the intake station asks Jillian.

"No, I'm his, well, girlfriend."

"Sorry, I can't give out any information on a patient to anyone who isn't a blood relative."

Jillian is all worked up. "At least tell me he's okay."

"I'm sorry," she says shaking her head. "It's the law. Why don't you take a seat and wait until we get clearance from his doctor for visitors."

"How long will that be? Never mind, I don't care how long it takes," she pledges and rejoins Josephine in a row of plastic seats in the emergency room waiting area.

"This is all my fault," Jillian says about to fall apart.

"Don't you even go there."

"He's supposed to fly to Phoenix this weekend. And now... everything is...this is a disaster," she cries, burying her face in her hands. Josephine rubs her back.

"Hey, I just saw the coach come out of the ER."

Jillian's head snaps up to see another lumbering man stroll out of the treatment room, talking with a doctor. "That's Uncle Jack," she says and makes a beeline over to him.

Unaware of what an emotional wreck she looks like, the men give her a weird look as she approaches them.

"You're Dallas's uncle, aren't you?"

The doctor and coach shake Uncle Jack's hand then walk toward the elevator. Dallas's protective uncle remains and looks at her suspiciously before answering, "Yes, and you're?"

"Jillian Miles, I live in the same apartment complex as Dallas. We're, um, good friends."

His eyes brighten and he smiles. "Yes, yes, he's mentioned you."

Her chest heaves a sigh of relief. "Is he okay?"

Uncle Jack's levity fades into grave concern. "Yes and no. He completely tore the rotator cuff of his pitching arm. It's a bad situation but not life threatening, thankfully."

"Oh God. Can they fix that?"

"He's going in for surgery soon when the swelling comes down, but the recovery will be long. Quite painful too, the doctor said."

"What about Arizona? Fall Ball and his big break?"

"Not going to happen. Truth is, and no one wants to say this out loud right now, but this injury just ended his baseball career. He'll never get his arm back for the majors...and probably not even for the minors."

Her face and shoulders sag, knowing how devastated he'll be from losing his passion. "Is he awake?"

"Not really. They have him pretty doped up to keep the pain and inflammation down. I'm waiting for the surgeon. If you'll excuse me I have to make a quick phone call before he comes."

"Of course."

Uncle Jack goes into a quiet corner with his cell.

Josephine meets up with Jillian. "How is he?"

"He tore his rotator cuff. They're scheduling him for surgery."

"Ouch. Oh, the poor thing. Keep positive, a lot of people have that operation and do just fine afterwards."

"A lot of people aren't pitchers in major league baseball, Josie."

"I know, honey. I know. Listen, I should give Gary a call and tell him what's going on. He'll be looking for supper soon."

"Josephine, go home. I don't want to make you hang around."

"I don't want to leave you alone."

"I'll be fine, really. Go home before he gets grouchy."

"You know how true that is. What about your car?"

"I can get a cab back to the ball field, don't worry."

"If you're sure...call me later and give me the update?"

"I will. Thanks, Jo." The women hug and Josephine heads out the emergency room doors.

An older doctor appears in the waiting room. The nurse behind the desk directs him to Uncle Jack who ends his call and greets the man with a handshake. The men head back into Dallas's treatment room.

Jillian takes in her the bland sterile environment. *There's nothing more timeless than a hospital hallway.* Even though she's exhausted, she can't sit down. She wanders the corridor and circles the waiting room too many times to count. Finally Uncle Jack and the surgeon emerge, finishing up what looks like a serious conversation before the doctor disappears in the elevator.

Uncle Jack sees Jillian and the two people who care about Dallas most converge.

"Surgery is set for day after tomorrow, seven in the morning. The surgeon thinks it was a clean tear so reattaching the tendons should go smoothly. If it does, he'll only have to stay in the hospital for a day or two at the most."

"That's good, right?"

"As good as we can ask for right now. The tricky part is the doctor said he can't go home alone, he'll need someone to help him with the shoulder gear and he won't be able to do much for himself. I've got tryouts on the West Coast that I can't miss. Hate to do it, but I'm going to have to find him a rehab facility for a few weeks until I get back. Damn his mother, the selfish bitch, excuse my French. She's my sister, I love her, but she should be here."

"It's sad she died so young. I'm sorry, it must've been so hard for Dallas and for your family."

"Died? Is that what he told you?" Uncle Jack shakes his head, but he's not surprised. "He never wanted to face the truth, still running from it."

"I don't understand."

"His mother isn't dead. She was having an affair with his varsity coach and Dallas was the one to discover it—literally by walking in on them. Next thing the kid knew, she packed up and took off with the scumbag in the middle of the night. Never said goodbye to him. He's never heard from her since, none of us have."

She puts all the pieces of Dallas's puzzle together in her mind. *Now it all makes sense. No wonder he can't let himself get close to anyone...his jealousy...Greg must've sent him over the edge. There's no one in the world who wants to take care of more than me. He deserves that, at the very least.* She tells Uncle Jack without a hint of hesitation, "No need for rehab, he can stay with me."

The big man is taken off guard by her offer, but grateful. "Are you sure? It's going to be a lot of work."

"I've never been more sure of anything in my life."

"Alright, alright. That would be super, thank you," he says. "Why don't you go home and get some sleep, there's nothing we can do here tonight. We'll touch base tomorrow," he suggests, handing her his phone number.

"Okay. Goodnight," she says and watches the large strong man walk out of the hospital, answering his phone.

But she has no intention of leaving without seeing Dallas. When the nurse isn't looking, she ducks into the emergency examination area and creeps down the hall until she finds him behind a partially-drawn curtain. The sight of Dallas lying in a hospital bed with tubes and a monstrous contraption on his shoulder breaks her heart. She forces the tears back as she nears the bed where the strong athlete she knows now looks more like a helpless boy. Unconscious from pain meds, he slumbers lifelessly in a white Johnny.

She sits in a chair next to his bed. There's nothing she can do, she just needs to be there. Her head throbs from a pounding headache and her eyes burn tired from all the crying. But she isn't complaining, it doesn't hold a candle to what Dallas is going through.

She stays, unaware of how much time passes, until an ER nurse enters to check on him.

"Visiting hours ended ten minutes ago, Miss. I'm sorry, you'll have to leave now," she informs her with compassion.

"I understand. Take good care of him, okay? Please?"

The young nurse smiles. "I will. He'll be asleep all night. You should get some too."

"Thank you," Jillian says genuinely appreciating the kindness in the RN's smile.

After kissing his cheek, she leaves, assured he will be in good hands.

# THIRTY-TWO

The nurse was right, she desperately needs sleep, but it isn't going to happen. Wired up from her emotional whirlwind of a day, her mind continuously replays the scream-fest between Dallas and Greg and then him rolling in agony on the baseball diamond. She needs to burn energy to pass out cold. Only way to do that is to do something physical. *The gym is closed, too dark for a walk. Wait, I know.*

Jillian laces up her cross-trainers and plops on her Cougars baseball cap. Grabbing Dallas's key and a variety of bags, she's off to his apartment to start packing up his stuff to move him into her place while he recovers.

While most of his belongings have never left their cartons, she does a weight test on all of them to determine which she can lift on her own and which are going to require hired help to move. After twenty minutes of this grueling workout, she finishes. She stands looking at the results; a small stack of the ones she can carry on now wait neatly by the door. The mountain of the ones that she can't, however, boggle her overtired mind. *I saw him lift all of these cartons effortlessly, but most of them are way too heavy for me to even budge. What the hell did he pack in these?*

Physical and mental exhaustion are creeping in and she pushes herself to at least do a little more before heading home. She tackles the bathroom, hurling everything into a large Ziploc bags. *Okay done. What next? Sheets and pillows. Should wash those too.* She stuffs the bed linens into garbage bags and folds his blankets. When she picks up one of his pillows, it infuses the air with his scent; his smell does her in. She falls apart, buries her face in his pillow, and succumbs to a good long blubber.

When it's all out of her system, she's more than ready to call it a night. Grabbing what bags she can carry, she shuts off the lights, and heads back to her own apartment to pass out and sleep like the dead.

# THIRTY-THREE

In the morning, Jillian arrives at the hospital right when visiting hours start. She learns from the hospital concierge that Dallas was moved out of the ER and into a regular room near the surgical wing. She wastes no time getting there.

His name is written on the placard outside a shared room, but is currently only occupant.

Jillian doesn't want to wake him but her footsteps betray her. He opens his eyes to see who is walking in. Love, hurt, and worry flood her chest when she makes contact with those beloved eyes.

"Hey," is all that comes out of her lips although there must be a million things she wants, needs, to say.

Immediately Dallas grows cold and anger makes him spits nails at her and his situation. "Get out of here," he spews, turning his face away from her in disgust.

Jillian can barely contain the tears threatening to fall from her eyes. "Dallas, we need to talk." She places a hand lightly on his leg. *We have to make this right. I'll do anything to get you to understand.*

He jerks his leg loose from her touch, but in doing so wrenches his torn shoulder. He groans from the sudden influx of pain. "Get the fuck away from me!"

The monitor by his bed beeps wildly. A nurse comes in to check on Dallas who tries desperately to find a comfortable position. "This sucks! Everything fucking sucks."

Jillian is in just as much pain watching him going through this and unable to comfort him.

"I'm going to get you some morphine. I'll be right back," the nurse tells him.

"Thank you. And take her with you."

The nurse shoots Jillian a questioning stare. The two women hold an entire conversation without a single word between them. The nurse smiles and walks out.

"Dallas, I'm not going anywhere until you hear me out."

He's not remotely interested in a word she has to say. He finally gets into a position that alleviates as much of his pain as possible and counts the seconds for his pain meds to arrive.

With nothing to lose and a completely captive Dallas Monroe, she pleads her case, "The last person on the planet I ever want to be with is Greg, you of all people know that. He showed up at my apartment unannounced, uninvited, to deliver some important legal papers. I pushed to get the funds from an old account we were closing in cash...so I can open my own restaurant. Because of you, your support and encouragement, I decided to go for it." Her words and underscored enthusiasm hang in the air and slightly melt the rigid block of tension between them.

The nurse reappears and gives Dallas a shot. "There, that should help. I'll be back to check on you in a little while," she says leaving the pair alone to surf a lingering frenetic silence.

Dallas, still not looking at her, hasn't reconciled it all yet in his head. He calls her on it. "He was half-naked, Jillian. Give me a break," he utters with a voice wanting to be proven wrong but clinging to a backpack full of doubt to protect his heart.

Knowing he just gave her a yellow light before a full green, Jillian seizes the opportunity to make things right and pulls up a chair by the side of his bed. She sits, wanting to reach out and touch him, but respects that they're not there yet.

"That was Mimi's doing. She hated him as soon as he barged in. After he helped himself to a glass of wine, your wine, she launched at him." Jillian covers her mouth to try to control her growing laughter as she replays it in her mind. "And she nailed him but good. Square in the chest. There was red wine all over his expensive white shirt." She lets go and howls over the event the way she wasn't able to at the time. The bubble of anxiety, worry over his injury, the stress of the misunderstanding between them, everything, feeds her laughing fit until tears roll down her face. "You should've seen the look on his face. Priceless," she says wiping the wet corners of her eyes.

Dallas, mellowed by the morphine and his unshakable belief in Jillian despite everything, starts to laugh along with her. "Mimi's my girl."

Jillian feels major relief having gotten that all out of her system. Dallas seems more at peace too.

"Hey, look at me," she requests in a warm loving tone, sliding her hand across the coarse wool hospital blanket onto his leg.

He does. His love for her emanates from his eyes which are now nearly consumed by narcotics. She sees every validation she needs from him swimming under those heavenly long lashes.

She gets up out of the chair and gently places her hand on his. The delicate contact with his skin is emotionally-charged tenfold.

"You know how I feel about you," she emphasizes as both a past reminder and present declaration.

He blinks his eyes yes. His face becomes serious and somehow more open than ever before. "Me too," he admits, clasping her hand.

They sanction their togetherness with an intense stare that is more powerful than any words.

She leans down and kisses his forehead. "You should get some sleep. I'll go take care of Mimi and Baxter and come back later, okay?"

He nods trying to stop himself from drifting off into an awaiting morphine slumber.

She whispers a promise into his ear, "I'll never leave you, Dallas. Not for anyone, not for anything." She lightly kisses his cheek then his lips. He closes his heavy eyes, safe in the fact that she means it. "Sleep," she says sweetly, giving him the permission she knows he needs to hear.

Jillian stays with him for awhile, watching him fall deeper and deeper into some far away painless dark place. Convinced he's okay for the time being, she tiptoes out of Dallas's hospital room.

# THIRTY-FOUR

"Guys, just stack those last ones, nicely, in the walk-in closet. Thank you," Uncle Jack directs a couple of Dallas's teammates who volunteered to help move their injured buddy out of his apartment and into Jillian's.

"I really appreciate the help. I was having trouble finding anyone who could come so quickly," Jillian says.

"And who aren't ex-cons," he remarks snidely.

The young strong men come back into the living room and stand with them to talk.

"That's everything," the short stop reports.

"You're sure?" Uncle Jack asks.

"Yep, that's it," the tall first baseman insists.

"Terrific. Thanks, guys," Uncle Jack says, shaking their hands.

"Give Dallas our best," one of the players says before they walk out.

"I guess we're done then," Jillian states, taking in all of Dallas's belongings in her living room.

"Not quite. There's one more thing," Dallas's uncle hopes he doesn't step out of bounds with his proposition.

"Oh?"

"I noticed you don't have a recliner."

Visions of her grandmother's 1970s reclining rocking chair dance in her head. Jillian's cheeks shrivel up like she's just eaten a sour pickle. "God, no. Why?"

"The surgeon said it would be best if he could sleep in one for a few weeks. It's going to be tough for him to get comfortable lying down after surgery."

"I don't know what to say. I can try to prop him up somehow. Maybe on the sofa?"

"If you don't mind the imposition, I'll have one delivered. It's the least I can do since you're kind enough to take care of him."

"A recliner, huh?" She peruses the apartment, swallowing her aesthetic pride as best she can. "Well, if we move that table I think we can fit one there. Maybe."

"The delivery guys will move whatever you need to move, I promise you that."

*What we do for love.* Jillian knows this would be the best thing for Dallas; she'll make peace with the ugly creature for him and his well-being. *Please don't let it be baby blue velour.*

"Try not to make it too, um, hideous. No offense."

"I'll have my wife pick it out, that should help a little," he promises which gets them both laughing. "I'm leaving for New Mexico this afternoon, please call me if there's anything, and I mean anything, you or Dallas need over the next few weeks."

"Will do. Thank you, Jack. Let's hope this goes as well as it can for him."

"Amen."

# THIRTY-FIVE

Dallas hungrily finishes up the beef tenderloin leftovers that Jillian snuck into his hospital room that evening. Like every television in Boston, his TV is tuned in to Game Seven with the hopes that the home team will win the coveted Pennant Race tonight. It's the bottom of the seventh inning and the Cougars are in the lead.

She takes the plastic container from him after he's eaten every morsel.

"That was so good, thanks. The food around here is pretty lame. How's the restaurant coming along?"

"There's so much to do, it's a little overwhelming. But in a good way. I gave my notice at work today. I have to be on site for work crews and deliveries. Sink or swim, that's my priority now. Of course, after you," she says holding his hand.

"That's huge. I'm happy for you."

Boston fans erupt with joy after St. Louis misses a chance to tie the game. The trailing Bishops call a time out and they go to a commercial.

"Who would've imagined when this series started we'd be where we are now? My life is on a completely different path thanks to you," Jillian says, upbeat.

"I'm glad one of us has a career to look forward to."

"Dallas, it's too soon to know anything. Think positive. Are you nervous about the surgery tomorrow?"

"Not really."

Crack! The sound of a fast pitch hitting a wooden bat pierces the room. Boston's best player has hit a home run out of Copley Stadium and all the men on base are hustling around the bases to home plate.

"What a play," Dallas praises the team. He and Jillian continue to watch the game and witness Boston up their big lead by four. "Hate to call it, but doubt St. Louis is gonna pull this one of the crapper."

Jillian is pleased. "Guess I win."

Dallas laughs at himself in his current state. "Yeah, I'm a real prize tonight," he points at his injured body. "Good luck with that."

"I have no problem waiting to cash in my win. Of course that means I do collect interest too...besides my special trophy."

"Sore winner you are," he jests. "But whatever you say, champ."

"Well, I might not be able to call in my win right now, but I am in the position of taking my trophy. Are you on?"

"Jilly, I've got nothing...unless peeping at a one-armed guy in a hospital gown does it for you."

"All you need to do is agree."

"I'm afraid of women who say shit like that," he jokes.

"Uncle Jack had to go out of town. We arranged it so you'll be staying with me for your recovery instead of a rehab center. Be my roommate?"

"You're sweet. But I can't."

"You've had better offers?" she gives him shit.

"No, of course not. But that's too...,"

"Committed? I know you're afraid of the c-word, Dallas. Listen, you got me out of my comfort zone, it's time you hauled your perfect sweet ass out of yours. My trophy. I won it fair and square. You can't say no."

He sighs, mulling it over. He gazes over at her, and gives in to what his heart truly wants: her. He decides to take a leap of faith and depend on her, get closer to her, even though it scares him to death.

"I guess I have no choice. I'm in."

She gets up and kisses him, careful not to disturb his bandaged shoulder.

"You're really something, you know," he murmurs.

A nursing student pops her head in the room. "Visiting hours are over in a five minutes," she says and disappears. You can hear her repeat the same message all down the hall.

"Good luck tomorrow. They won't let me see you before surgery, but I'll be here. I'll see you as soon as you come out of recovery."

"That means a lot to me," he admits.

"I wouldn't be anywhere else in the world tomorrow. We're no longer Boston and St. Louis, Dallas, we're a new team. Our team. You, me, Baxter, and Mimi."

"Sounds like World Champs to me," he says fist pumping her with his good hand. "Go home, gorgeous. I'll see you tomorrow on the flip."

# THIRTY-SIX

Everyone Jillian's ever worked with at Phasitech over the years gathers in the cafeteria to celebrate her going on to follow her dream. Josephine cuts a devilishly-tempting chocolate cake. She hands Jillian the first piece.

"Did you get this from Sin City?" Jillian asks, licking the frosting off her fork.

"Where else? Their pastry is better than foreplay," she claims.

"Not sure about that, but it's pretty close," Jillian laughs. "Thanks, Josephine."

"Honey, we're going to miss you around here in a big way. But don't you worry, I already told Gary we'll be regulars at your restaurant every Friday. You're not getting rid of me that easily."

Russ swoops in and grabs a plate of cake before it's all gone.

"What's the name of your place, Jillian?" a co-worker asks with Russ and her other colleagues standing nearby wolfing down the sweet cake.

"You know, that's been the hardest part. I don't know yet."

Russ puts in his two cents, "They say a business name should be personal. Something that has meaning to you or else it sounds generic and feels cold to the public. Especially a restaurant, I would think, right? Don't make it sound like a franchise."

"Good advice, thanks."

Each of her well-wishers, now flying on sugar highs, say their goodbyes and vanish one by one.

Josephine starts cleaning up the empty paper plates and tries to keep up a strong facade, but Jillian detects her sadness. They've been constant office buddies for years. And more than that, good friends.

"By the way, I didn't get a chance to ask you, how did Loverboy do in surgery this morning?"

"It went as well as can be expected. He's really out of it, which is a good thing. It killed me to see him like that in the recovery room."

"I'm surprised they're keeping him. For most hospitals now it's outpatient surgery and then they kick you out to the curb. Health insurance companies are such bastards."

"The tear was that bad, that need to monitor him. He's going to have a tough road ahead. The next few weeks are going to be hell."

"You'll take good care of him," she says, taking a last look around for trash. "Well, I guess that's it." Josie ties up the last garbage bag.

"Thank you for everything, Josie," she says. "I'll miss seeing you every day."

"Me too, honey," she replies teary-eyed. The friends hug.

Josephine, true to form, regains her spunk quickly. "But I have to look on the bright side, now I'll have more wall space in the cubicle for The Hoff."

Jillian laughs. "Then my quitting is a win-win situation for both of us."

# THIRTY-SEVEN

Two weeks post-surgery, Dallas leans back in his leather recliner talking on his cell with Uncle Jack. With his right arm in a bulky sling, he's pretty much all done with the disabled routine. He hasn't left Jillian's apartment since the operation and he's going stir crazy.

"I appreciate it, Uncle Jack. I'll think about it, really. It's a great offer, I just need to get my head around a desk job. It's been awhile. Okay, talk to you on Friday."

"What was that all about?" Jillian asks coming out of the kitchen and falls flat on the couch, wiped out from her day at the restaurant.

"I am so jealous you're able to do that," he tells her.

"Do what?"

"Lie down."

"Soon, Dallas, soon. You're doing great."

"Yeah, just peachy. Anyway, Uncle Jack offered me a management job."

"That's great, isn't it?"

"I'm thankful, of course, but man, I haven't done nine-to-five in forever. And the truth is I don't know if I can work around baseball if I'm not playing. I'll be reminded every second I blew my shot. But then again, what other job can I do? I'm not really qualified for anything else."

"When do you have to give him your answer?"

"End of the week. I'm sure I'll take it. Just have to sort it out in my head first, that's all. Enough about my tales of woe, how'd it go at the restaurant today?"

"Busy. Total chaos with construction crews and interviewing people for wait staff. But I loved it. I was wondering if you feel up to seeing it tonight?"

"I'd love to! Let's go. I need to get out of here for awhile, no offense. And I've been dying to see your dream taking shape. Picked out a name yet?"

"Yes, finally," she is pleased to report. And happy with her decision. "The sign guy was coming by after I left. I haven't seen it yet."

"Let me guess, it's called "Jillian's"?"

"Nope. You'll see."

"Ready when you are."

With worry and care she helps Dallas get into the passenger seat of her car. The safety belt over the sling is tricky but they make it work. She drives slowly out of the lot, trying to avoid driving over any bumps that might jostle his healing shoulder.

By the time they reach the upscale neighborhood in Chestnut Hill, the sun has set. She pulls up in front of her building and smiles when she sees her restaurant's name written across her door in an elegant script.

"Dandelion? Where'd that come from?" Dallas asks totally surprised by her choice.

"It's kind of a family inside joke," she says and leaves it at that, not needing to explain to him that he in fact is her precious dandelion, one that she wouldn't trade for an ocean of roses in bloom.

Helping him out of the car is easier than getting him in. Excited to show him everything, the moment they step inside she watches his reactions like a hawk. Just like her, the first thing to grab his attention is the intricate mahogany bar. He immediately goes over to it.

"This is unbelievable," he exudes approval and admires the fine workmanship. "This is going to be one hell of a bar."

"I'm so glad you like it, Dallas."

"What's not to like?"

"Good. I'm hoping you'll consider running it for me."

He peels his eyes away from the liquor shelves to look at her. "What?"

"This has the potential to be the best wine bar in Boston. I need you, your expertise, to run it. I know it's not baseball, but with you at the bar and me in the kitchen, we'll have a really great business here."

Dallas is taken aback by her proposal. He walks around the counter and inspects every portion of the antique bar set up. He likes how it feels to be back there; it gives him a particular kind of enthusiasm he hasn't felt in a long time. He loves wine, sharing wine, tending bar. And to do it side-by-side with Jillian?

"You're on."

"Oh, Dallas. Thank you. This is going to be amazing!"

"No, Jillian, thank you. I can't wait to get started."

"Me neither. Let me give you the grand tour then we'll go home and I'll show you the menu I've been working on so you can start thinking about pairing wines."

He walks back around to where she's standing, running his hand over the top of the varnished bar. He then extends it to her, pulling her towards him after she accepts it. Carefully, strategically, they maneuver around his sling to come together for a kiss.

# THIRTY-EIGHT

A month passes when on a Sunday afternoon, Dallas, now out of his sling and doing pretty well thanks to physical therapy, rests on the sofa with his laptop ordering bar supplies. A football game is on TV and the dogs are chasing each other around the apartment.

"Calm down, you guys," Dallas warns without taking his eyes off the computer screen.

Baxter follows Mimi who hops up on the back of the recliner to peer out the window. The two dogs snuggle up together, watching the world outside go by until Mimi starts to bark. Then Baxter chimes in.

Jillian, in the kitchen making lunch, grows annoyed by the nonstop canine racket. "What is going on in there?" She yells to Dallas while drizzling a kale salad with a fresh citrus ginger dressing.

"Beats me, they see something outside," he yells back. "Must be a cat."

Jillian pauses and smiles. *Must be.*